DOUBLE FRAME

DOUBLE FRAME

A Sam Quinton Mystery

KEVIN R. DOYLE

Kenmore, WA

A Camel Press book published by Epicenter Press

Epicenter Press
6524 NE 181st St.
Suite 2
Kenmore, WA 98028

For more information go to:
www.Camelpress.com
www.Coffeetownpress.com
www.Epicenterpress.com
www.kevindoylefiction.com

Cover design by Scott Book
Design by Melissa Vail Coffman

Double Frame

ISBN: 978-1-68492-012-9 (Trade Paper)
ISBN: 978-1-68492-013-6 (eBook)

Printed in the United States of America

To Tom O. and Kelly S., who gave me a shot at career redemption. Hopefully, I didn't let you down.

CHAPTER ONE

In the middle of a Monday afternoon I was working on the arms, doing concentration curls, when a good-looking older woman stepped into my gym, The Blaster.

That in itself wasn't unusual. Mainly due to the efforts of Lisa Nolan, my manager, The Blaster, despite its name, has become something of a Mecca in the Providence area for women, both middle-aged and gracefully edging beyond, to come work out. And because most of them tend to work hard at keeping in shape, they usually veer toward the good-looking side of the equation.

This particular woman, however, didn't appear at all in the mood to work out. Instead, her eyes made a quick circuit of the place, making note of the scattering of clients engaged in all sorts of planned, strenuous activity, then alighted on me, off in the corner and doing my curls.

Even from across the room I could see her nod her head briefly, as if confirming something to herself, then make a straight line in my direction.

Somewhere, by my guess, in the late forties, she wore black slacks and a charcoal-gray sweater with burgundy argyles, perfectly complementing both the gloomy March weather outside and her thick black hair, which held only a few streaks of gray. She obviously didn't see the need to color her hair, and giving her a quick appraisal, I found myself in agreement.

I put down my dumbbells and waited for her to come over.

When she did, she stood fidgeting for a moment, her look of cool poise drooping a bit.

When she got close, I could see her eyes were a striking royal blue color.

"Mr. Quinton?"

"That's me." I grabbed a water bottle from underneath the bench I was sitting on and took a swig.

"I'm interested in hiring you," the woman said.

"I don't do individual sessions," I said. "I can take you over to talk to Lisa Nolan. She handles most of our formal scheduling, and I'm sure—"

"No, I," the woman paused, took a breath and shook her head a trifle. "I'm not looking for a trainer."

"Aah," I said, the light dawning.

"I need a detective." She peered closer at me while keeping her expression blank. I was wearing gym shorts, a tank-top tee shirt, and white Puma's. My face was still a little flushed from the curls, and at the end of a one-hour workout I probably needed a shower.

"Pardon my appearance," I said. "I wasn't expecting to see any clients this afternoon."

The woman looked around, her gaze sweeping the gym, before coming back to me. "You are a detective, aren't you?"

"Yes, I am."

"Then I need to hire you."

I perked up at the word "need," not "want." "What sort of work?" I asked.

She frowned as she looked down at me. "Detective work. That is what you do, isn't it?"

I shook my head. "What I meant was what sort of case. What do you need help with?"

Her face crumpled a bit, and a hint of moisture seeped into her eyes. She shook her head slightly, and I wondered if she was going to turn around and head back out the door.

Then she took a deep breath, squared her shoulders and stood up a little straighter.

"My name is Susan Thayer," she said. "Does that explain the kind of work I need?"

"Thayer."

"Correct."

"As in Dr. Felix Thayer?" I asked.

She nodded, and looking closely, I could see two parallel tears sliding down her cheeks.

Oh yeah. I don't know if that explained everything, but it explained an awful lot.

CHAPTER TWO

A FEW MINUTES LATER WE WERE IN MY OFFICE, me sitting behind my desk and Susan Thayer in one of my client chairs. I'd grabbed a bottle of water out of my mini fridge, but she'd declined any sort of drink.

Sitting, she almost shimmered, still giving off that sensation of barely-contained emotions.

"Judging by your reaction out there, I'm assuming you've heard of my husband," she said.

"Same as anyone who's paid any attention to the news the last few weeks. Professor at the university accused of killing a co-worker in a fit of professional jealousy? Who wouldn't hear about that?"

"I want to believe that my husband's innocent," she said.

I took a deep breath and placed my hands flat on my desk. More than once I've had to explain the facts of life to stubborn clients, and it was a job that never got easier, no matter how much practice I had.

"According to the cops, he killed Michael Hartness."

"Felix disliked Michael. Everyone knew that. But I find it hard to believe he killed him."

"Been my experience that the police usually get this sort of thing right. Your husband have a lawyer?"

A tremor ran through her, and I again wondered at the amount of self-control she was exerting. "Yes," she said, sounding as if she had something caught in her throat.

"What's wrong with him?" I asked.

Susan Thayer gripped her hands together, her fingers turning almost white with tension. "His name's Daniel Lancaster, and I'm sure he's perfectly competent, but he only passed the bar three years ago, and my husband hired him for a murder case."

The name wasn't familiar to me, but that didn't exactly mean anything. Even though Providence's population was in the low six figures, that still left room for an awful lot of lawyers to clutter the landscape. I agreed with her, though, that it was unusual for such an inexperienced lawyer to take on something this major.

"Lancaster do any work for the city or state before going into private practice?" I asked. "Maybe the PD's office?"

"Not as far as I can tell. I googled him, of course, but didn't find much. Only a couple of dry legal references."

"He work for a firm, or on his own?"

"As far as I can tell on his own. I know it sounds crass on my part, but he comes off as pretty much a rock bottom attorney."

I thought about that for a few seconds. "How are you and your husband doing financially?" I asked.

A brand-new stiffness came over the lady's features. "How does that matter?"

"Well, for one, I'm wondering if you'll be able to pay my bill. More to the point, though, I'm wondering if this Lancaster fellow is all you guys could afford."

The stiffness eased, a little, but most of it remained. We stared at each other across my desk for a couple of heartbeats before she slumped back in her chair.

"We're doing very well financially. More than well enough to hire the best. But I'm afraid Felix doesn't quite see it that way."

"Ah hah," I said.

"Ah hah?"

"Means I'm guessing most of the family money comes from your side."

"In which case, you'd be guessing correctly." For the first time since she walked up to me in the gym, she showed the barest trace of a smile. "It's true that Felix is paid decently at the university, but yes. There's money on my end as well."

"Are you guys rich?" I asked.

"It depends on how you define rich. We could at least afford to hire a much more experienced lawyer."

"And your husband's too proud to use your money."

Another pause while she smoothed her hands down the front of her skirt. "I don't know if proud would be the correct word, and in fact we never discussed it. I've always seen it as our money, but I can't imagine any other reason for him to hire someone so—so green—for something this important."

"What exactly is it you want me to do?" I asked. "Work with his lawyer? Try to prove him innocent?"

"Not exactly." Those eyes began to swim again, but once more she got it together before losing control. No matter her circumstances, I had the feeling I was in the presence of one hell of a woman.

"You don't exactly want me to work for his innocence? Pardon me, Mrs. Thayer, but I'm a little confused."

She took a deep breath, pulled herself up straighter. "I want to know the truth."

"I noticed you'd been speaking kind of conditionally all along."

She nodded. "I'm doing everything possible to support Felix, but he's not the most—amenable—of men, as I'm sure you'll find out when you start digging around."

"Okay."

"If he's innocent, if this is all some huge mistake, I'll support him all the way through."

"And if he's not?" I asked.

"I'll deal with that when the time comes. Either way, I have to know."

"Why not just let the police do their investigation? After all, that's what they're paid for. And they have a whole lot more new, shiny tools than I do."

"Mainly because it seems they've already made up their minds. Granted, the evidence against Felix seems almost beyond overwhelming, but that's part of my confusion."

"Meaning?"

"Meaning that, if I stretched it, I can see my husband murdering someone, but not the way they say he did."

"That's not exactly a ringing endorsement for his innocence," I said.

"Let me put it this way. Felix can be—volatile—at times. But not physical. He's an academic, for God's sake, and ordinarily his bark is much worse than his bite. And if he did go as far as to get violent with someone, he wouldn't do it so obviously."

"According to the news, if I remember correctly he bludgeoned Dr. Hartness to death with a paperweight, then left both the weapon and his blood-soaked clothes in his office at the university."

"That's my point. The Felix I know is one of the brightest men I've ever met. I can almost believe him guilty of murder, if in some way he were pushed too far. But such a blatantly stupid murder? That just doesn't make sense."

I thought about it for a few minutes. If nothing else it sounded like an interesting case, but I wasn't sure I could do all that much, either way, to ease the woman's peace of mind.

"How are you going to explain my presence? After all, if I start nosing around for you, the good professor's going to know about it in no time. The second thing I'll have to do is talk with him."

She focused her gaze squarely on me, a bit of fire returning to those stark blue eyes. "Felix will just have to deal with it. If he makes a fuss, I'll throw it right back at him and explain that I hired you on my own, using my funds."

"And with your funds, you can afford my bill?"

Now the fire was replaced with just the slightest hint of amusement. "Yes, Mr. Quinton. Trust me. You won't go hungry working for me."

"In that case, I'll consider myself hired."

We spoke a little bit longer about the mechanics and finances of her being a client before Mrs. Thayer stood up to go. "I'm curious," she said.

"About?"

"You said that talking to Felix is the second thing you have to do. What's the first?"

I grinned at my new client. "Get the official version," I said.

CHAPTER THREE

"YOU START WORKING FOR CREEPS LIKE FELIX THAYER, you're going to get a bad reputation around here," Josh Nichols said.

It was an hour or so after Susan Thayer had left my office. I'd showered, changed into somewhat decent clothing, and headed downtown to the central police station. Providence is a small enough city that we have only the one main station downtown and a couple of little satellite facilities scattered around the outskirts.

I'd gone up to the second floor, which held the detective squad room, to check in with Josh Nichols. He was detective sergeant, on a force as small as ours basically the second in command, and his desk was situated closest to the enclosed office of the head of the squad, Lt. William Santiago.

"I know," I said, "but got to pay the bills somehow."

"Come on, Blondie. What kind of bills can you have that would require taking on a client like Thayer?"

I smiled. "Maybe I just needed something to do. The way Lisa's running the gym, I'm beginning to feel like a fossil around there."

"Not quite the mousy little waif you took under your wing a few years back?"

"Hell, Josh. If I don't keep an eye on her, she'll end up owning the place in another six months."

Nichols stared at me for a moment. He was in his early thirties with a few more lines than he should have at his age.

Then again, the guy has a tough job.

I glanced over at the enclosed office with the frosted glass panels. "Lt. Santiago in today?"

Nichols glared at me. "What difference does it make if the lieutenant's in? I'm the one in charge of the case."

I smiled at my buddy. "Thought I'd pop in and say hello. You know, shoot the breeze a bit. Swap stories about him brushing shoulders with the boys in Chicago and me hanging out with the pro wrestling greats."

Nichols grimaced and looked down at the file spread out on his desk. "There's no such thing as a great in pro wrestling, and even if there was you spent most of your time in the minor leagues."

"Says you."

"And the lieutenant never talks much about his time in Chicago."

"You ever wonder about that, Josh?"

"No. I like my job too much."

I shrugged. "Even so, I'd like to say hi to old Bill."

"You do know that the lieutenant judges you somewhere below toenail fungus, right Blondie?"

Nichols was one of the few people I didn't mind calling me Blondie. The nickname's a holdover from my ring days, when I went by the moniker of The Blond Bomber. I'd first met Nichols back when he was a young patrolman for the St. Louis P.D. supplementing his income by doing security gigs for the Midwest Wrestling League.

"If that's what your boss thinks of me, means I've done something lately to move up in his estimation," I said.

"Uh huh." Nichols bent down and scanned the file documents again, though I was sure he knew them by heart.

"Paper files, Josh? Haven't you guys moved up to the digital age yet?

Nichols grimaced. "Digital is for people who don't have to move their lips while they read. Last I knew, that didn't include you."

"That mean you're going to let me read the file on my own?" I asked.

"And have you sit here all day taking up space? Don't think so."

I took a closer look at Nichols, wondering about the uncommon surliness of his attitude. His shirt was rumpled, and he had some dark rings around his eyes.

"Here's what we've got," he said after a few minutes. "Late afternoon eleven days ago, a graduate student at the university found the body of Dr. Michael Hartness, assistant professor of sociology. He'd been bludgeoned repeatedly with a blunt instrument, and there were indications he'd been choked as well."

"Means he died hard," I said.

"Betcher ass he did. There was blood from the head wounds splattered on his office floor and ligature bruises around his neck."

"Sounds like someone with a lot of physical strength."

"Or someone who was really pissed at the man."

"How does Felix Thayer fill that bill?" I asked.

Nichols looked at me for a second. "You haven't met him yet?"

"Nope. Figured I'd swing by and get the official version from you, then talk to the guy and find out what really happened."

"Hah, hah. Let's just say he'd have to have fallen into the really pissed category."

"Not a lot of physical strength there?" I asked.

Nichols shrugged. "Looks about what you'd think a sociology professor would look like."

"Okay," I said. "The weapon?"

"Round obsidian paperweight that the vic had on his desk."

"Vic? Come on, Josh. Stop watching those *NYPD Blue* reruns."

"Hey, you asked."

"That handles means. What about opportunity?"

"They worked in the same basic office complex. It's a central space with five separate offices branching off of it."

"So there'd be another three or four possible suspects," I pointed out.

"Except that we found *the vic's* blood spattered all over your client's shirt."

I considered pointing out that Dr. Thayer wasn't exactly my client but figured it would come off as quibbling. "You searched his house?" I asked.

"Didn't have to. The shirt was wadded up and thrust into one of the drawers in the filing cabinet in his office. Plus, there were visible blood spatters on Thayer's desk and the arms of his chair."

"Motive?" I asked.

"According to everyone who worked around them, the two hated each other."

"Josh, they're professors at a university. All of those folks hate each other. Haven't you heard the old saying about the stakes in academe?"

"No, and I don't want to. You still dating that secretary from the campus?"

I gave him my sheepish grin. "We go out every now and then. What about alibi?"

"Why don't you ask your client?"

"Because I'm sitting right here with my good buddy, who has the goddamned file opened up in front of him."

Nichols grinned, though it had a kind of mischievous aspect to it. "Says he was right there in his office, quietly working, through the whole thing."

"Anyone to back that up?" I asked.

"You ever been in a college office on a Friday afternoon?"

"Means no one to back it up."

"Not unless we get around to interviewing some of the cockroaches, no."

"Let's recap, then," I said. "You have two faculty members who don't get along, one of whom ends up beaten to death with a paperweight, and the other says he was a few feet away and didn't hear anything, but there's no one around to support that."

"Don't forget the bloodstained shirt and the blood in Thayer's office."

"Prints on the paperweight?" I asked.

"Only in your dreams. With all the blood and gunk smeared over the thing, there's nothing to pick up."

"But all the clues point like a neon sign to Thayer?"

"That's about it."

"Josh," I said. "You're describing probably the stupidest coverup of a murder ever."

"Then your guy's stupid. Not my fault."

"He's a Ph.D.," I pointed out.

"Not synonymous with smart," Nichols said.

The guy had a point there. "Still," I said. "It sounds kind of whacked to me."

Nichols put the papers down and gave me a long look. "Before you make any judgements, why don't you go and actually talk to the man? See what you think of him."

"That's my next step."

"I give it five minutes, ten at the most, before you want to kill him yourself."

CHAPTER FOUR

I DECIDED TO MAKE A CHANGE IN MY GAME PLAN and check out Felix Thayer's lawyer next.

Downtown Providence stretches all of about twelve city blocks in length and two or three in width. Not a large city by any means, though we have about anything one would want in their town. Main Street runs the twelve blocks in length, and almost all of the buildings are no more than three stories tall. Once upon a time, a city mandate held that no building could be more than five stories at the most, but after enough pressure from developers who wanted to flood the area with apartments for student housing, that rule got overturned.

The developers got their wish, and they immediately started a flurry of construction that resulted in droves of apartments priced at over a thousand dollars a month that could only be rented by young people who belonged to the upper, upper class, which led to a downtown populated almost exclusively by twenty-year olds.

Just imagine what that's like on a weekend night.

At the northwest corner of Sixth and Main rests one of the older buildings, two stories in height. A men's clothing store occupies the bottom floor, with most of their inventory so expensive I think I've been inside a total of once in the time I've lived here. The top floor is divided into two sections, with a narrow hallway in between. On one side is an Italian restaurant, and on the other is an office with a plain wood door with the words lettered: "Daniel Lancaster, Attorney at Law."

Walking inside, I found a small, spare outer office, one with a secretary's desk but no secretary present, a couple of brown leather easy chairs, and a small metal coffee table with a couple of old magazines scattered on it.

There was also another door, cracked partially open, on the opposite side of the room.

"Hello," I called out.

"Just a minute," came from the other side of that open door, and a few seconds later a man appeared.

He was of the right age, early thirtyish, around six feet tall, skinny and with a thatch of already-thinning brown hair. He wore a gray two-piece suit that looked fairly new and a bright maroon tie. I wondered if I'd caught him either coming or going, or if he wore the suit jacket in his office all the time.

He looked me over, an expression of faint distrust showing on his face.

I get that a lot.

"Can I help you?"

"Mr. Lancaster?" I asked.

"Daniel Lancaster, yes. And you are?"

"Sam Quinton." As far as I could tell, the name didn't mean anything to him. I opened up my wallet and showed the photostat of my investigator's license.

Reaching into his jacket pocket, the attorney pulled out a pair of reading glasses, put them on, and peered at my license.

"Nice to meet you, Mr. Quinton, but if you're looking for work I'm afraid—"

"I'm here to talk to you about Felix Thayer."

"Aww." Lancaster nodded. "Susan must have sent you." I noticed a faint twang in his speech and wondered if he were originally from the southern part of the state.

"Can we talk in your office?" I asked.

"Certainly."

He ushered me in, and I saw that his personal office was pretty much as threadbare as the reception area.

Then again, my office is in the back of a gym. Who am I to talk?

"I've heard of you now and then, Mr. Quinton," Lancaster said. "Generally fairly good stuff, but I'm not sure what Mrs. Thayer expects out of you."

"Basically, she wants me to see whether or not her husband is a murderer."

"I understand, but that's my job, isn't it?"

"No. Your job, as I'm sure you know, is to try to get him acquitted, guilty or no."

"But Mrs. Thayer wants the truth, no matter what. Correct?"

I gave him a smile. "There's a few things that are bothering her about all this."

"I've no doubt. But anything beyond the obvious?"

"Well, for one, she's wondering why Dr. Thayer hired you."

A couple of seconds of dead silence followed that one, as the two of us stared each other down. Finally, Lancaster squirmed a little bit, and a slight sheen of sweat appeared on his forehead.

"I guess she thinks I'm a little inexperienced."

"Is she right?"

The lawyer clasped his hands together on his desk. "I've been practicing for four years."

"Many murder cases in that time?"

Those clasped hands got a little tighter. I felt like hell for needling the guy, but I had to get some basic facts on the table.

After a minute of tension, he seemed to collapse a bit and fell back in his chair. "No, sir. None, in fact. I've defended a couple of clients on felonies, mainly robberies and assaults, but nothing that rises to this level."

"You can see why Mrs. Thayer's a little concerned for her husband's prospects."

"I can. However, just because I'm new at the game doesn't mean I'm incompetent."

"Of course not," I said. "I think her main question has to do with why, considering their resources, Dr. Thayer picked someone at your level for representation."

"I've actually wondered about that myself. You're aware there's some family money on Mrs. Thayer's end?"

"She made that pretty clear when we talked."

A flicker of a smile crossed Lancaster's face. "I'm guessing you wanted to make sure you'd get paid."

"I did indeed."

The grin became more than a flicker now, and I had a feeling the ice had broken between us. "When he came to me, Dr. Thayer made it fairly clear that his wife's money is off limits to him. He has his salary from the university and what he can make from articles, books, speeches and the like, but whatever she brought into the marriage is strictly hers."

Now it was my turn to frown. "Funny, that's not the impression Mrs. Thayer gave to me."

"How so?"

"According to her, she considers what's hers to be his as well."

Lancaster joined me in frowning. "For some reason, that's not the way Felix sees it."

Okay, chalk up at least one inconsistency. There could be something to explore there.

Then again, it could simply be the age-old issue of couples not clearly communicating about money.

"You have any problem with me nosing around on this?" I asked.

"Not at all. I'd only ask that if you come across anything validating his innocence I know it before the cops do, even if only by an hour or so."

"I can live with that. What about if I come up with evidence for his guilt?"

The attorney thought about that one for a minute. "I guess the more informed I am altogether the better it will be. I assume you're aware that I'm not obligated to relay any information that argues for my client's guilt."

"I am. But I need you to be aware that anything I find, no matter what, goes to the cops. As I said, Mrs. Thayer didn't ask me to prove her husband innocent. She asked me to find the truth."

Lancaster didn't look comfortable with that, but there really wasn't anything he could do. "As long as we know where each other stands."

CHAPTER FIVE

MY THIRD STOP FOR THE DAY WAS THE CITY JAIL.

After a couple of minutes of the usual song and dance of getting in to see an accused person, I was sitting down behind a plexiglass screen as they brought the supposed murderer in.

He was wearing a regulation jail jumpsuit, one baggy enough to make him seem even scrawnier than he probably was. Even in the jumpsuit and after several days in stir, he had an air about him. He walked into the room and looked down at me with a haughty expression.

He sat down in front of me, stared for a second like I was a bug under a microscope, then lifted up the black plastic phone.

"Who are you?" were his first words.

Despite his incarceration, Felix Thayer carried himself with the air of a man about to begin a lecture. He was somehow clean shaven, and his dark brown hair, hanging just below his ears, looked as if he'd just stepped out of a salon.

I guessed the guy cared about his appearance.

He looked as if he'd been in decent shape once, an avid tennis player maybe or perhaps racquetball, but had slacked off for a couple of years.

Although he wore gold-colored wire frames for his eyes, up close I could tell the lenses were clear glass, meaning he obviously wore them for appearance's sake.

Interesting thing to note. If he was looking to play the role of entrenched academic, it could mean he was a somewhat deceptive person in other ways as well.

"My name's Sam Quinton. I'm a private investigator."

"You working for my lawyer?" He peered at me through the glasses.

"No. For your wife. She hired me to help you out."

Some stretching of the truth there, but I figured acceptable under the circumstances.

Thayer leaned back in his chair and studied me, his eyes looking owlish. I guessed he wanted me to feel like one of his students who'd scrambled into class five minutes late.

"Hired you to do what?"

"I would assume prove your innocence. Dig around and find evidence that you didn't kill Michael Hartness."

"That's what I have a lawyer for."

"A lawyer who's a tad—young, shall we say."

"According to you."

"I notice he didn't manage to spring bail for you."

Now Thayer grinned, but there didn't seem to be a whole lot of humor in the expression. Looking at him, I could almost envision him as the kind of guy who'd get pleasure out of kicking a puppy out of his way.

"I really don't see how who I hired for legal counsel is any concern of yours, mister. Why don't you go find some bar to throw drunks out of? By the look of you, that's about all you're qualified to do."

And here I'd worn my nicest peacoat to come see him.

"Maybe, but as long as I'm here, and you're here, why don't we put our heads together. Heck, if nothing else, how could it hurt to talk to me?"

Now the man gave me a bit of a snarl. "Let's get this straight, mister. If, or when, I go to trial, I'm going to be able to beat it on my own. I'm not going to need any lowlife to help me out."

Under the little counter that runs in front of the plexiglass I was clenching and unclenching my fist.

"You said 'if.' You doubt you'll go to trial?"

"I'm hoping that these asswipe rent-a-cops we have in this town will come to their senses before then."

The guy was a sweetheart, for sure. I was starting to seriously wonder what a woman as classy as his wife saw in him.

With my free hand, I drummed my fingers on the counter in front of me. "How about humoring your wife, Mr. Thayer?"

"That's Dr. Thayer." His voice went up about half an octave in my ear. "The least you could do would be to address me with the honorific I've earned."

"Yeah," I said, unable to tolerate the guy any longer, "but you earned it in sociology, so that doesn't really count, does it?"

Thayer steamed at me for a couple of seconds, then stood up and slammed his phone on the hook, hard enough it bounced off and slammed onto the counter. One of the guards standing by the door began to edge his way.

A minute later, they'd hustled the professor back to his cell, while an older woman wearing a plain blue dress stood behind me, waiting to sit down in my place.

Judging by the scrawny, strung out guy coming up to the chair Thayer had just vacated, eyes darting every which way and cords popping out in his neck, I guessed the old woman was going to have an even worse conversation than I'd just had.

CHAPTER SIX

I WAS SITTING IN MY OFFICE LATE THAT NIGHT, working on some minor paperwork, when the desk phone rang. I stared at it for a minute. Since Lisa Nolan had taken on so much of the running of the gym, it was rare for me to get calls at any time, let alone at night. And while we were still open for another hour or so, available to late shift workers who wanted to let off steam, it was way too late for a business call.

I picked up the phone.

"Sam," Keri Eckland, our latest hire who likes working the late shift, said, "there are a couple of men heading toward your office."

"What kind of men?" I asked.

"Well, I don't think they're here to work out. I asked if I could help them when they came in, but they brushed right past me and headed your way."

Before I could respond, my door opened and three men walked in.

"That's okay, Keri," I said. "I've got it." I hung up the phone and examined my visitors.

The guy walking in front was slightly under six foot and looked in pretty good shape. It was somewhat hard to tell, as the thousand-dollar suit he wore under an open camelhair overcoat was no doubt tailored to hide any imperfections. I pegged his age at somewhere in the mid-fifties.

He had sandy blond hair, beginning to go thin, and bright blue eyes.

The two men flanking him looked like typical thugs, dressed up in suits and ties, at eleven at night no less, but thugs all the same.

They stopped about three feet inside my office, the one on the left closing the door behind them.

"You Quinton?" the blond asked.

"I am," I said, "and I know why you're here."

"You do?"

"Of course. You're interested in the six-month special we're running, the one where you get to work out five days a week and consume all the gunpowder shakes you can handle."

The blond sighed and, without being invited, sat down in one of my client chairs. The two flankers backed up a couple of steps and arranged themselves on either side of the door.

Probably expecting me to become overcome with fear and make a run for it.

"I heard about you," the blond said. "They tell me you're better than you come off."

I smiled and spread my hands modestly.

"You know who I am?" the man asked.

"Not for sure," I said. "But if I had to take a guess, I'd say you're probably Sean O'Flaherty."

"Then you are smarter than you look."

"Only on days ending in a y," I said.

Shaking his head, my visitor crossed his leg at his knee. His two companions still hadn't moved from the door.

"You know why I'm coming here to see you?" he asked.

I shrugged. "Not really. Unless you want me to teach your lackeys there a few pointers so they get better at beating up Girl Scouts. Or possibly they need better tips on tailing someone without being noticed."

Sean O'Flaherty chuckled. "Lackeys. That's a good one. You know these lackeys would tear you apart if I as much as said boo."

"I know they'd probably try. But there's a long gap between trying and succeeding."

"Maybe they're the men to span that gap."

"Maybe, then again maybe not."

Sean O'Flaherty nodded and relaxed back in his chair. "You've interested yourself in the affair of Dr. Felix Thayer." He didn't state it as a question.

"Maybe," I replied.

"Then maybe you should uninterest yourself in said affair."

"Then again, maybe not."

O'Flaherty showed the slightest indications of burn around the edges of his jaw. "I'm starting to think you're not very smart. If you really knew about me, you wouldn't be quite so disrespectful."

I sighed and leaned back in my own chair, my foot resting on an open desk drawer. "I know you're the latest, prettiest face that the mob's sent in to run Providence. I know that you've taken over most of what's left after my old friend Paddy O'Brien bit the dust. I know that you think you're all that, when in reality I'd guess that Chicago's keeping you on a really short leash."

Now the red had begun to creep past his jaws and into his cheeks. Behind him, the two stiffs were picking up on their boss's mood and tensing up themselves.

"Maybe you don't know as much as you think," he said.

"Could be I know more. What I don't know is what interest you have in the Thayer case."

"I would think it's enough that I have an interest," O'Flaherty said.

"Not to me."

The crimson flared even more for a moment as the bodyguards got edgier, then O'Flaherty calmed down, and a slight smile cracked his face. "Despite your appearance, I'd heard you were a smart guy. Now that you've guessed it, wouldn't you say it's a good idea to back off?"

"Not really," I said as I slouched even lower in my chair, closer to that open desk drawer.

"Meaning you'd side with a flake like Thayer over doing me a solid?"

"If he was still alive, I'd probably side with Sadaam Hussein over you. Nothing personal, but lately this town has had about all the Irish gangsters it can handle."

The smile vanished, and O'Flaherty stood up, the two men behind him coming to attention. "I'm trying to deal straight with you, Quinton, but it seems you're just too much of a showman to let it go. Do what you think's best, as long as you're ready to deal with any fallout that comes your way."

"I'm just trying to figure out why a mob guy is willing to go out on a limb for a college professor he doesn't know. Doesn't add up to me."

O'Flaherty sighed and reached into his coat pocket. I tensed up. He pulled his hand out a moment later and plopped a wrapped bundle of bills on my desk. "See if that adds up."

I used the edge of my hand to nudge the packet sidewise. The top bill was a fifty, and the packet was about an inch thick.

"I'm guessing that equals out to about three month's worth of pay, provided you worked every day, which from what I understand you don't. So how about you take that dough and do whatever you want. Sock it in the bank, go on a cruise, buy all brand new equipment for this dump. Whatever, as long as you stay out of the Thayer business."

I nudged the packet again, this time edging it back in the mobster's direction. "Don't think so," I said.

O'Flaherty shook his head. "You really going to turn down all that money?"

"This may be a hard concept to grasp, Sean, so I'll talk real slow. I already agreed to look into the case, and I took someone else's money before yours. Much as I'd like to double my yearly income in five minutes, I think I'm going to have to decline."

As I spoke, I lowered my right hand closer to the desk drawer.

A long, slow minute drug by until O'Flaherty grimaced and picked the money up off the desk. "I heard you weren't too bright, Quinton, but I didn't expect you were this dumb."

"You going to have your cousins there get rough with me?" I asked.

He paused, as if contemplating just that, before standing up and staring down at me. "Maybe in another day and time, yeah. But this isn't the old days, and the bosses back East are still trying to get this part of the state under control since Paddy bit the big one. They wouldn't think too highly of any sort of ruckus, at least for now."

I realized I'd been holding my breath for several seconds and took in a small sip of air.

O'Flaherty turned to head out the door, then paused half over the threshold and looked back at me. "Just be careful where you step, Quinton. The solid ground under you can become quicksand real quick."

And with that, my visitors were gone.

I took in more air, considered for a minute, and came to the conclusion that no, I wasn't really trembling, then closed the desk drawer, where my gun had hovered inches from my fingers.

Now, I had two mysteries to solve. One, did Felix Thayer really kill his office mate in the stupidest manner imaginable?

And, possibly just as important, why the hell did the local mob care about a dispute between two academics?

Far as that went, how the hell did they find out I was working on the case the same day I started?

CHAPTER SEVEN

The next morning, I met Josh Nichols at a coffeeshop close to downtown. He had a plain black, while I had a touch of cream and sugar and a cinnamon bear claw.

"Black?" I asked, "Don't you want to live it up a little?"

Nichols, already looking slightly rumpled at seven in the morning, grinned. "You know all those old jokes about cop shop coffee?"

"Yeah?"

"Trust me, they're all true. Plain black is a pure luxury compared to the swill I usually have to have at work. Plus, you're buying."

"Beauty of getting to charge expenses," I said. "You should try it sometime."

"I've got news for you, buddy. What's called expenses in private enterprise is considered bribery if you work for the city."

"Oh, yeah. I forgot about that."

"To what do I owe the pleasure of this fine coffee and your company this morning?"

"I had a talk with Sean O'Flaherty last night."

Nichols gently put down his cup and stared me full in the face. "This the first time you guys met?" he asked.

"Yep."

"What'd he want?"

"Wanted me to get off of the Thayer case."

Nichols frowned, placed his elbows on the table and steepled his chin in his fingers. "Come again?"

"Wanted me to stop working for Susan Thayer. Even threw a big pile of money on my desk to get me to lay off."

"Which I'm guessing you refused to do," Josh said.

"Something like that."

"He get rough?"

"No. Had a couple of bully boys with him, and conceivably something could have ended up happening, but he seemed to want to take the high road. Made it very clear, though, that I was not welcome in the Thayer matter."

"Shit," Josh said.

"My thoughts exactly. There goes your nice, clean, no-strings-attached homicide. You come across anything in Thayer's life that would link him with a wannabe goombah like O'Flaherty?"

"No, unless you count his tendency to be an annoying prick to everyone around him. It's possible that he crossed paths with the Sean Man at some point and pissed him off, but we haven't heard about it. Then again, we weren't really looking for anything like that."

"No reason you should have." I paused to take a bite of my pastry. "What about Hartness?"

"Come again?"

"Seriously, Josh, keep up with your case. Dr. Michael Hartness? You know, the victim?"

"Of course, I know. You mean any mob ties on his end?"

"That's exactly what I mean."

"Again, we weren't looking for anything like that. He was a professor, for Christ's sakes. We'll check it out, but there's a flaw in your theory there, good buddy."

"I know," I said, almost positive that Nichols and I were thinking along the same line.

"Let's say there's something shady in Hartness's past, and God only knows what it could be. But just for the hell of it, let's say Sean O'Flaherty, or someone connected with him, did Hartness in."

"Okay, let's say."

"How in the hell did he get on to you so fast? How'd he know you were even working on this?"

"I didn't say I'd thought it all the way through, Josh. Even so, how about giving me the lowdown. Is O'Flaherty for sure taking over Paddy's action?"

Nichols nodded and reached over with a fork to take a piece off my bear claw. Considering I was on expenses, I let him do it. I could always get a second one.

"Far as we can tell, he's Chicago's man on the scene in all ways here."

"What about St. Louis?" I asked. "They're a lot closer."

"True. But ever since all that shit went down with Don Lipardo, St. Louis doesn't have all that much clout anymore. Everything west of the Mississippi is basically Chicago's turf now."

"I'll take your word for it. Last night notwithstanding, I do my best to stay away from those guys."

"Doesn't quite add up, though," Nichols said.

"How so?"

He finished chewing his bite and took a swig of coffee before answering. "When Sean showed up, naturally we looked into him. The police out there sent us everything they had on the guy, or at least everything they said they had."

"What doesn't add up?" I pressed.

Nichols took another drink. "The guy's a real up and comer. Hell, you met him, Blondie. Young, smart, looks good. Of course, they're never going to take him into the brotherhood. He's not the right ethnic line. But from everything we can see, the Outfit guys like him and were grooming him for major stuff."

I leaned back in my side of the booth and stared at the ceiling for a minute while I processed all that.

"Am I correct in guessing," I said after a few minutes, "that Providence and the surrounding area is considered pretty small stuff by the power guys?"

"You are."

"But the state capitol's down the road."

"It is," Nichols said, "but come on, man. Everyone around here knows that the real power centers in the state, what's left of them, are Kansas City and St. Louis. And if we know it, you can for sure bet Chicago knows it as well."

"Then why," I asked, "would the big boys send one of their fair-haired wonder kids down to take care of such a piss poor territory?"

Nichols cocked his hand into a gun formation and made a shooting motion in my direction. "That's what we've been trying to find out for a while. So far, we haven't come up with a single viable reason."

I thought about it a little more. "Maybe we can go at it another way, Josh. Instead of why is O'Flaherty here in general, what's his interest in the Thayer matter? Is there any reason he or his guys would have taken out Hartness?"

"That doesn't make sense, Blondie. Even if they had, why the hell would they go to the trouble of framing Thayer for it? The boys don't work that way. They would have just scooped him up, taken him somewhere, and put a bullet in his head. The way it went down, a whole lot of extra trouble, and for what?"

"Yeah," I said. "It is kind of a long shot. But there was some reason O'Flaherty came to see me. Some reason he wants me to walk away from it. I just don't know what the hell it is."

"Whatever the reason," Nichols said, "you'd better figure it out real quick."

CHAPTER EIGHT

After leaving Nichols, I sat in my car and pulled out my phone. The night before, I'd worked out a basic plan of action, which included beginning at the top with the university chancellor.

Amazingly, after only one phone call I got an appointment with him for ten o'clock. His administrative assistant told me the chancellor had about twenty minutes in between a deans meeting and heading down to the state capital for a pow wow with the governor, making me feel giddy all over that he'd elected to take the time to talk to little old me.

I decided to dress up for the occasion. Since the weather was in full-blown March mode, I put on a long-sleeved chambray shirt and dark blue wool blazer as I headed out to meet the big man.

Turned out, not all that big.

The assistant, a thirty-something black woman named Lila, dressed impeccably on a Kohl's budget, ushered me into the inner sanctum. I'm not sure what I expected a chancellor's office to look like, but it was understated, with a lot of dark wood, somber colors, and two trellised windows closed against the weather outside.

Dr. Raymond Withers stood up and held out his hand across a desk about three times as large as mine back at The Blaster.

I'd seen Dr. Withers on the news a time or two and occasionally sitting in his box when I'd attended this or that game at the university stadium, but I'd never been up close and personal with the man, leaving me a little astonished that he stood only about five foot six.

Combined with his weight, that I judged somewhere north of two hundred very soft pounds, he didn't exactly come across as an imposing, fearless leader.

"Have a seat," Withers said, gesturing toward two chairs in front of his desk, dark leather with black wood frames. I took a seat, leaned back and crossed one leg over a knee.

Withers sat back down behind his desk. "So," he said, "you're working for Felix Thayer."

I nodded.

"Why exactly did he need to hire a private detective?"

"Probably to help prove his innocence," I said, deciding not to tell him that Thayer's wife was my actual client. Not really a lie, but then again it wasn't exactly any of his business who was paying my freight.

"That's a pretty large leap to make, isn't it?" Withers asked.

"The leap being?"

"That the man's innocent. After all, the evidence against him is pretty overwhelming."

I resisted frowning, though it wasn't easy. "I would assume as a scholar that you would be willing to evaluate all the evidence and not make a snap judgement."

Now it was Wither's turn to frown back at me as he tried to raise himself a little higher in his chair. No matter how much he stretched, though, he couldn't make his five-six come anywhere close to my six-two.

"Don't be confused about my role here, Mr. Quinton," Withers said. "As an ordinary citizen, I of course subscribe to the concept of innocent until proven guilty. And if I were an ordinary person assigned to his jury, I'd most certainly keep an open mind, but as the leader of this institution, I have other considerations in mind."

"Such as keeping bad publicity down to a minimum?" I asked.

"That's one consideration, yes." Withers took a moment to stroke his chin. I guessed that at some point in the past he'd sported a goatee.

"And it doesn't help recruitment, not to mention donations, to have a murderer with tenure, right?"

"You're more aware than you seem, Mr. Quinton. And you're correct. This institution has several stakeholders, and it's my best assumption that none of them are pleased with this little scandal that's broken out."

Little scandal. One prof killed and the other arrested for the crime. I wondered what, in his world, constituted a major scandal.

"But wouldn't it be worse," I asked, "if Dr. Thayer turns out to be innocent and you all turned your backs on him?"

Withers leaned back and spread his hands across his desk. For a moment, he looked at the far wall of his office, almost as if looking through it to the other offices beyond, and past that to the entire campus grounds, before focusing back on me.

"I'm going to be frank with you, Mr. Quinton, but if you utter publicly anything I'm about to say, I'll deny it as vociferously as possible."

I nodded but kept my mouth shut. I'd learned before that when people want to talk it's best to let them, whether you end up believing what they say or not.

"Felix Thayer," and the chancellor spoke slowly enough that he almost drawled, "was about the most hated person on our campus."

I thought of contradicting his use of the past tense, seeing as how the man hadn't even gone to trial yet, but abstained. "Considering that between students, staff and faculty you've got something close to forty thousand people here, that's quite a statement."

Withers grinned, and for a second he appeared almost likeable. "Not quite forty thousand, but you're essentially correct. We have a larger population than most of the cities in this state."

"And out of all those, young and old, male and female, Democrat, Independent, socialist and even, when they slip past the radars, the occasional conservative, Thayer takes the prize as most hated? By whom?"

Withers steepled his fingers together and assumed his professorial demeanor. When I got back to the gym, I'd look up what field he'd taught in before heading into the upper levels of university administration.

I was pretty sure it wasn't phys. ed or basket weaving.

"Take your pick," he said. "He was feared by his students, despised by his colleagues and resented by the hourly staff."

"Wow!" I said. "And all that before he's even a full professor."

The grin of a second before returned, only now it widened into an almost smile. "Despite you're trying to present a thuggish exterior, Mr. Quinton, I'm going to guess that you're well aware there are very few who reach that high of a rank."

"I barely made it through high school, doc. Wouldn't even have done that if the neighborhood cop hadn't made me his personal project and kept corralling me off the streets and back into the classroom."

"Education, or lack thereof, is not necessarily synonymous with intelligence."

I started breathing a little deeper, steadying myself. I was beginning to think that my initial assessment of Dr. Withers was way off. "Let's start with students," I said. "Why did they fear him?"

"Probably because he was—is the most unreasonably harsh grader I've ever seen in nearly thirty years in higher education."

"Tough to get an A, huh?" I said.

"Actually, damned near impossible to get a C. Felix has single-handedly wrecked more grade point averages among sociology majors than anyone else in the department."

I frowned.

"Tell me this, Dr. Withers. If he was that impossible in the classroom, how'd he ever stick around long enough to get tenure? Granted, from what I understand performance in the classroom is the furthest thing from consideration when you decide whether or not to keep someone around, but even so . . ."

Now it was Withers's turn to frown. "Mr. Quinton, if you're going to continue insulting my profession, I'd say this conversation is at an end. Let me point out that I didn't have to see you, considering who your client is, and I'm doing this as a favor. Are we clear?"

When you've faced off with as many tough guys as I have, staring down a university chancellor doesn't present that much of a challenge. Even so, the man had a point, and pissing him off wouldn't get me the information I wanted.

"Sorry, doctor. You were saying?"

Withers relaxed a fraction of an inch. "Actually, though, you do have a point. Especially in the social sciences, research and service is much more heavily weighted when it comes to personnel decision. But classroom performance isn't exactly out in the desert."

"Which means my original question had some validity," I said.

"It most certainly did. Unfortunately, I can't divulge the inner workings of specific personnel decisions to outsiders."

"Is there any kind of upcoming decision having to do with him?" I asked. "From what I understand, once someone has their tenure they're basically set for life."

"Again, Mr. Quinton, I can't get into those kind of matters. Though your understanding of the tenure process is, more or less, correct."

I caught that "more or less" clause, but decided not to push it at the moment. "Do you know of any particular animosity between Thayer and Hartness?"

Withers smiled. "Really, Mr. Quinton. Think about how many faculty and staff we have at this institution. I can't be expected to know the intimate details of all of them."

Not exactly a denial. Again, for now, I let it go.

"I got that. But can you tell me this. Other than students, was there anyone else Thayer had a problem with?"

Withers waved his hand almost dismissively. "It would be simpler, and quicker, to tell you who didn't have issues with him."

"Oh yeah?"

"Most definitely. His colleagues distrusted him, primarily because of unproven allegations of stealing their work. He treated the hourly staff like his own personal servants. I have reason to believe he's tried on occasion to harass the administrative staff. Do you need me to go on?"

I shook my head. "Considering your earlier reticence," I said, kind of proud of myself for coming up with that word, "I'm wondering why you're being this forthcoming right now. I'd think, if for nothing other than legal reasons, you wouldn't be quite so open."

The chancellor smiled and peeled back his shirt cuff to look at his watch, even though when I entered the room I'd noticed a clock on the wall opposite of where he sat.

"Maybe I hate to see a man waste his time and effort defending a lost cause," he said.

"Sure, that could be it."

"Or maybe I despise Felix Thayer as much as everyone else, and if you report any of this conversation it's merely the word of a university official against that of a—pardon me—professional snooper."

"Even more likely," I said.

CHAPTER NINE

After getting the perspective, what there was of it, from the top as to the life and times of Felix Thayer, I decided to go at things in a more horizontal fashion and walked across campus to Bevier Hall, a large building that housed the H. R. Murton College of Social Sciences, which in turn housed the department of sociology.

The university, founded somewhere in the late 1830's, had been continually and successively added on to for most of the time in between. As such, it's a sprawling campus that serves as home to students numbering in the tens of thousands. Because the development, as usually happens, wasn't performed in a smooth, progressive manner, you can find brand spanking new buildings, mainly of glass and metal, elbowing up against brick constructions that look like they are part of the original load that came by barge across the Mississippi.

Bevier Hall was one of those older buildings, and as I walked in and sought out a directory pinioned in a far corner of the first floor, I figured that, in this case, older was better.

At least this structure looked, felt and smelled like a school, which was more than I could say for some of the other buildings around the campus.

Then again, my appreciation for the older stuff may have something to do with the fact that I'm a lot closer to fifty than I want to be.

Sociology, as it turned out, was on the fourth floor. I climbed the stairs and went through a door on the right that had a small sign with Thayer's name and four others, half expecting to see one slightly-large room with desks for all of the professors.

Instead, I walked into a small anteroom with a counter, a small desk slightly behind the counter, and behind it five office doors arranged in a horseshoe.

A black woman was seated at one of three chairs behind the counter.

"Can I help you?" she asked, looking away from her computer as I entered.

"Hi," I said, "my name's Sam Quinton."

"Hello, Mr. Quinton. How may I help you?"

"Well, this is going to sound odd, but I was wondering if I could talk to someone about Felix Thayer."

"Uh huh." She stood up and came to stand at the counter in front of me.

Her age was hard to pin down. The backs of her hands were a little tight and shiny, like those of an older woman, but her body was slim, strong and, clothed in a maroon skirt and dark gray turtleneck sweater, gave the appearance of someone who kept themselves in shape.

She had short hair tightly curled around her face, strong cheekbones and full lips. Her face appeared unblemished, but that could have just been good makeup.

"And who did you want to talk to about Dr Thayer?" she asked.

"Whoever's available."

Without turning away, she waved a hand at the five closed doors behind her. "Everyone's either in class or out for the day. Including Thayer, but since you're asking about him, I'm guessing you know why he's not around today."

I smiled as widely as I could. I thought about giving her a sly, knowing grin, but decided she'd take that the wrong way.

Or maybe the right way.

"What can you tell me about the good doctor?" I asked.

Now it was her turn to smile, though I sensed a touch of ice behind it. "And why should I tell you anything? What is your business anyway?"

I pulled my wallet out of my pocket and showed her my license. She took one quick glance, then a longer look.

"A private detective? For real?"

"For very real," I said. "Don't I look like one?'

"Depends on ones expectations, I guess," she said, and I noticed a little more education slipping into her speech. "To a regular person, no. You don't really look like what they'd think. But do you ever read Connelly?"

"Huh?" I asked.

"Michael Connelly. The Lincoln Lawyer books? You look exactly like the detective in those."

"Good to know," I said.

"Yeah." She smiled again, all the ice gone. "Except that guy's better looking. And cooler."

"But he's fictional," I pointed out, trying not to appear crushed.

"A girl can dream."

I didn't have a quick response to that one, but I did the best I could. "And just who am I talking with here?"

Her smile became broader. "My name's Felicia Adams. I'm the faculty secretary around here."

"Since you're working at a progressive, upscale university, shouldn't you say 'administrative assistant?'" I asked.

"I should," Felicia Adams said, "if I cared about that kind of crap. What is it you want to know?"

I glanced at the desk she'd been sitting at when I first came in. "Am I keeping you from anything important?"

"Not unless you call proofreading Dr. Shipton's latest grant request important."

"It isn't to me," I said.

Felicia Adams smiled. "Me either."

"What does a faculty secretary actually do?" I asked.

Felicia shrugged. "Officially, I perform any and all administrative operations that the tenured faculty of the department require."

"And unofficially?"

Felicia glanced at a clock on the north wall. "It's about time for my break. You on expenses?"

"Far as I know."

Now I got a dubious look. "Well, does your massive expense account have enough to buy me a cup of coffee?"

"I think I can swing that."

"Then get your wallet out, bubba, 'cause after the day I've already had I could use a jolt of caffeine."

"It's not even mid-morning," I pointed out. "How hard could your day have been so far?"

"Harder than you'd believe."

CHAPTER TEN

THAT LATE IN THE MORNING, the coffee lounge we picked wasn't that busy. The university's big enough that it holds probably two dozen eating places, food kiosks, fast food outlets and coffee spots. You can get practically any sort of food or beverage desired somewhere on campus, but we had decided to settle with just plain coffee.

At least I did. I had regular with a bit of sugar added in, but Felicia Adams had one of those godawful, foot-tall, sugary concoctions that go by three or four different Italian names. As we sat down I looked closer at her drink and figured that actual coffee only made up, at the most, fifteen percent of the brew.

"You're not afraid to be seen with me?" I asked as we sat down with our drinks at a corner table.

"Should I be?"

"Well, I am investigating Dr. Hartness's murder. And with Felix Thayer as the main suspect, some people may talk."

"Let them talk away," Felicia said. "What will they think I'm doing, giving away state secrets?"

"I've been wondering myself."

"Maybe I'm trying to further the cause of justice," she said. "After all, you are trying to find out the truth, aren't you?"

"I guess. At the moment, I'm not all that sure what's expected of me. Cause of justice sounds like a possibility, though. How would you go about doing that?"

Felicia grinned. Her teeth were even and straight, except for one slightly crooked eyetooth. "Who do you think knows more about all those profs than the person who screens their calls and visitors? Handles their snail mail?"

"Valid point," I said. "And you'd be doing this because?"

"Because maybe I want to make sure the truth comes out."

"What's the truth about Felix Thayer?"

"That he's about the biggest douche I've ever met. And I grew up in the bad part of town and had an abusive boyfriend once upon a time."

I shook my head. "You're too mature and put together to use a word like douche."

She grinned even harder. "Hey, if the bag fits . . ."

"Care to be a little more specific?" I asked, my conversation with Chancellor Withers still fresh in mind and wondering how much the two versions would match up.

Felicia took a sip, probably to compose her thoughts. "For one," she said, "he treated me like an eighteen-year old freshman."

"Meaning he looked down on you?"

"Looked down on, ordered around, even tried to get me to fetch his coffee my first day on the job."

"How'd that go?"

She giggled. "After about half an hour he gave up on waiting and came out of his office to get it himself."

"Okay, he wasn't that hot of a boss. So what?"

She began ticking off her points with her fingers. "He was rude, especially to students, or really anyone he saw as lower than him. He flirted with practically anything in a skirt or high heels, the younger the better. He tried to steal work from his colleagues, which isn't that big of a thing as they tried to steal it right back from him."

"So far everything you've said pretty much lines up with what my other sources have told me."

"What other sources are those?

"Sorry," I said, primarily because I didn't think it would be professional etiquette to let anyone know the top guy at the university had spilled his feelings about one of his faculty. "Got to protect them."

Felicia shrugged and took a sip of her coffee. "Doesn't really matter," she said. "Everyone knows what a flake the guy is."

"And why aren't you worried about talking to me?" I asked. "After all, it could cost you your job to be talking bad about the profs here."

"Doesn't bother me. I've only got a couple of months anyway, then I graduate and am out of here."

"Degree in sociology?" I asked.

She gave me a withering look that, had I not been as tough as I am, might have shrunk me to the ground. "God, no. Who would want to be in that field?"

"So your area is . . ."

"Psychology," she said with another beaming grin. "Makes a lot more common sense than soc does."

"I'm guessing you're a late bloomer?" I asked.

"Uh huh. Married at nineteen, had a kid at twenty. After I got rid of the no-good boyfriend, married a marine instructor who up and got killed during a training accident, of all things. My boy just graduated college last year and is doing a year of missionary work in Kenya. When he was about halfway through his degree, I realized that before long I'd find myself an empty nester and would need something to do." She held her arms out wide, palms up. "So far, this is the something."

I smiled. "Then why're you being chatty and friendly with me? After all, I may end up digging up some of the department's dirty laundry."

Felicia shook her head. "I figure it like this. On the one hand, Thayer killed Hartness and nothing you do's going to change that. On the other hand, someone else did it and up to now has gotten off scot free. Which means we may just possibly have a killer roaming around the campus."

"Makes sense."

"And I may be wrong, but you don't impress me as the kind that's going to pull every dirty trick there is to get your guy off even if he's guilty. You strike me as having a little more integrity than that."

"Your psychology training tell you that?" I asked.

"Nope. My over four decades of life dealing with men tells me that. Ergo, if Dr. Thayer really is the killer, won't hurt any to help you because in the end he'll still get what's coming to him."

"And if he isn't, I may just possibly find the real killer and make the streets of Providence a little safer."

She held up her coffee cup in a sort of mock salute. "You bet. Plus, there's the actual main reason for helping you out."

"Which is?"

Felicia looked around at the nearly empty cafeteria. "Don't know if you noticed it or not, but spring break's right around the corner, and it's boring as heck around here right about now."

CHAPTER ELEVEN

I SAT AND TALKED WITH FELICIA FOR a while longer. By the time we were done, I had a fairly clear idea of the direction I wanted to take in my investigation. I walked her back to her desk in Bevier Hall, then made my way out to my Cherokee. As I sat there with the motor and heater running, I pondered my next move as I watched a few stray, crispy white snowflakes flutter down.

I had just begun the information-gathering stage of things and was already wondering if my initial move, beginning at the top, had been the right way to go. But that was where I'd begun, and it made a certain kind of sense to keep pursuing that direction. Fortunately, because I'd had Felicia to fill me in on how things worked around the place, I knew that after starting with Chancellor Withers at the top, the next step down would be the dean of the social sciences department, which covered everything from psychology to criminal justice.

The dean, it turned out, did not have an office in Bevier but in another building halfway across campus. I glanced at the time. Right around noon on a weekday, the odds of catching Dr. Talia Sanderson in her office were slim, but at the moment I had nothing else to do. And once you've picked a direction of investigation, it's better to stick with it rather than run pell mell all over the place.

It only took about five minutes to get the distance across campus to the dean's office. Felicia had been right. Although school was still technically in session, between the cold weather and spring break looming in a week or so, the place was practically deserted.

I found a parking slot right in front of the building I was looking for, made my way inside, consulted a directory off to the right of the doors and ran up the stairs to the second floor.

All the doors were closed except for one. Glancing at the nameplate above, it read "Dr. Talia Sanderson, Dean."

Good thing I'm trained as a detective, or I may not have tracked her down.

Glancing in the doorway, I saw a small outer office and a door on the opposite side, that, I assumed, led to an inner office. That door also was opened about halfway, and light shone from inside.

"Hello," I called out.

"Come on in," came a strong, modulated woman's voice from the inner area.

I made my way back and, despite the opened door, knocked once on the jamb.

"It's open."

As I walked in the office, I went over everything Felicia Adams had told me about Dean Sanderson. It wasn't a lot. She was supposedly middle age, had been in education her whole life, and sometime in the past decade or so had worked her way up into administration.

I steeled myself, expecting a female version of Chancellor Withers.

What I got was something else instead.

"Yes?" The woman sitting behind the desk looked up as I walked in.

She was a blond, somewhere in her late forties, possibly fifty, with green eyes and prominent laugh lines around her mouth. She wore a harvest green skirt and black V-neck sweater, and when she stood up to greet me, I couldn't help but notice that she kept herself in great shape.

"Dr. Sanderson?" I asked.

"Yes?"

I showed her my license.

"Aww, yes. I've been expecting you." She gestured towards one of the soft chairs in front of her desk.

"Word about me getting around already?" I asked as I sat down.

Dr. Sanderson smiled, which caused her laugh lines to crinkle. "Chancellor Withers called about an hour ago. Said I shouldn't be surprised if a big, thuggish-looking man came to see me."

"Thuggish-looking? Has he shown up yet?"

Another laugh, and more crinkling. I controlled my breathing so I could keep focused on my job.

"What can I do for you, Mr. Quinton?"

"I'm kind of fishing," I said. "Trying to gather as much info as I can about Dr. Thayer's job, relationships around here, whatever I can find."

"And how does that help his case?"

"Don't know yet. But the more I learn, the more I know."

She nodded. "I'm sure Chancellor Withers made clear that we have to honor certain confidentialities. I would guess someone in your business can understand that."

"I can, but I was wondering if there's anything that wouldn't fall under that umbrella?"

"You have to understand that I don't work day in and day out with either Felix Thayer or Michael Hartness."

"But I'll bet you have, or had in one case, more interaction with them than Withers does."

"I do, and did." Again with the eye crinkle.

"Anything you can tell me?"

She mulled that one over for a minute, which I didn't mind. Gave me more time to sit there and look at her without coming across as a creepizoid, as Lisa Nolan would say.

Finally, though, she shook her head.

"I'm sorry, Mr. Quinton. But I really don't think there's anything I care to divulge."

"Then there is something?" I asked.

"Excuse me?"

"You may not want to tell me, but there clearly is something more here about those two."

She smiled again, though a little less brightly than previously. "Have a good day, Mr. Quinton."

I nodded, smiled back, stood up, and left.

CHAPTER TWELVE

WEDNESDAY MORNING, I SHOWED UP bright and early at the university, hoping to have time to speak to the three professors who shared the office suite with Thayer and Hartness. However, I'd overlooked one basic flaw in my plan.

Namely, the bright and early part.

As I walked into the common office area around eight thirty, it hit me right away that I should have checked with Felicia Adams the day before as to when exactly all those bright minds showed up to work.

Because the closed office doors indicated they might not show up when regular people did.

On the other hand, Felicia was already sitting at her desk, tapping away on her computer. She looked up and smiled when I came in the door.

"Back again?"

"Sure," I said, staring intently at the closed doors. "I'd hoped to catch the other professors today for some light questioning. Are they all in class or something?"

Felicia laughed, a deep, full-throated sound that spoke of total amusement. "You really don't know much about how this world works, do you?"

"No, but I'm willing to learn."

"If only I had the time to teach you, which I don't. Cliff's Notes version, dude. Dr. Lawrence shows up every other day around noon, shuts the door and does God knows what until shortly after two, then leaves."

"Doesn't he have any classes to teach?" I asked.

"*She* usually does, but this semester they've given her time to work on a new book."

"Okay."

"Dr. Schumacher is low man, or person, on the totem pole, which means he actually makes it in about three days a week."

"Let me guess," I said, "for a couple of hours each day."

"Actually, no. He has class each of those mornings, gets in the office around eleven or so, and spends most of the day in there working."

"You sure he's an academic?" I asked.

"It's what the nameplate on his door says."

"Is it possible he's, oh I don't know, dedicated to his job?"

"Dedicated's probably too strong a word," Felica said after a moment's thought. "Let's just say he doesn't view working at a public university as a glorified form of welfare."

"Fair enough," I said. "That leaves one, right?"

"Right. Seeing as how one of the original five's dead and your client probably did it. That leaves Dr. Shipton."

"He or she?" I asked.

"Oh, most definitely a he." Her voice had developed a tinge of aggression.

"In terms of?" I asked.

"In terms of thinking he's God's gift to the science of sociology, and that any other field of study is inferior at best, tawdry at worst."

I grinned. "And in your time working here, have you had the opportunity to discern Dr. Shipton's views of your own field?"

"I sure have," she said, a note of finality in her tone.

I decided to switch gears. "And when does Dr. Shipton show up?"

"Whenever he darned well pleases, but most weeks he wanders in late Thursday morning."

"Another gone-by-noon type?" I asked.

"You got it."

I took a moment to consider things. Any sort of competent investigation would include interviewing the people who spent time in closest proximity to either the deceased or the suspect, which in this case would be both. Therefore, it really was kind of necessary for me to talk to the other three professors in the office.

And I needed to do it even if the cops had already interviewed them. By the time Nichols and his team had gotten around to talking to the profs, they already had their suspect locked up and, intentionally or not, would have narrowed the focus of their questioning to confirm what they already had pretty much proven.

I didn't consider this any sort of indictment of the cops or their methods; I was merely looking at it from their point of view. They had a suspect, his bloodied clothes still in his office and the murder weapon hiding in his desk drawer. Didn't take a genius to figure out the way the wind was blowing.

My approach had to be from a more skeptical point of view, which meant I could possibly come across things the cops hadn't.

At the moment, though, none of the officemates were around. I could run all over town tracking them down, and would probably have to do just that, but seeing as I was already in the building, a more practical short-term approach seemed obvious.

"You know what would help me," I said to Felicia, "would be to inspect Thayer and Hartness's offices."

Felicia leaned back in her chair and looked up at me. "Mr. Quinton, you're kind of cool, and I like you and all, but I really don't think I should do that. The police would probably object."

I glanced behind her to the array of closed office doors. "I don't see any crime scene tape," I said. "They're not sealed off or anything, are they?"

"No." She drawled out the single syllable quite a ways. "They actually were done in here the other day and packed all their stuff up."

"So?"

She shook her head. "I don't think the university administration would care for it, either. From what I understand, you already had a talk with Chancellor Withers that could have gone better."

"It didn't go all that bad," I said. "And how'd you know that anyway?"

"We're a large campus here, but in some ways we're like a small neighborhood."

"Meaning word gets around?"

She nodded. "Especially among the administrative staff."

"Still . . ."

"Uh huh. You and he got along swell, right?"

I smiled even bigger. "Not as well as I did with Dr. Sanderson. So how about those offices?"

Felicia got up and began moving some papers around on her desk. "Funny thing," she said. "I'm not positive, because I haven't had a reason to worry about it, but I've got this feeling that when the cops packed everything up, they didn't bother to lock Dr. Hartness's office."

"They probably figured that with it being one of a suite, and an alert guardian like you at the portal here, there was no reason for it."

"Could be," she said. "On the other hand, could just be that they got careless. Either way, I'm not for sure it's unlocked, but it could be."

She reached into her center desk drawer and pulled out a key. She idly tapped it on the desk a few times before laying it square in the center.

"I've got to run over next door and drop off some material for one of the TA's," she said. "Probably be gone a while. Far as that goes, it's nice enough out this morning that I may just take a walk around campus. You know, stretch my legs."

"I always say early March in Missouri is the perfect time for walking outdoors," I said.

"Ain't it, though?" Felicia said as she walked from behind her desk and headed out the door. She stopped in the doorway and half turned back.

"By the way," she said. "If you look closely, there's two keys there on my desk. Leaving stuff laying out like that. Guess I'm getting careless in my old age."

CHAPTER THIRTEEN

I MADE SURE TO SHUT THE DOOR behind me. Despite what Felicia had said, there was no telling when one of the other professors, or anyone else for that matter, would decide to drop into the suite, and the open door would be a dead giveaway that something was up.

After shutting it, I leaned against the door and surveyed the entire room.

Not a whole lot to see, actually.

A desk about three feet long, wood with a white trim. Black tubular chair behind it and small red couch ranged along the opposite side. Two tall metal cabinets on the wall to the right of the desk and three small, old fashioned filing cabinets, three drawers to each, painted green and against the other wall.

Two windows that looked out on the grounds to the east of the building, equipped with half-angled venetian blinds.

A thin, almost unnoticeable, atmosphere of dust hung in the air.

The cops may have packed up their equipment and left, but traces of the crime remained. Dried brown stains spackled the light beige carpet. Similar stains decorated the baseboard on the wall behind the desk. The desk itself sat slightly askew, as if it had been jostled in the struggle and never straightened. Same with one of the tall cabinets ranged along the wall. It still stood upright, a little out of true with the wall.

And, of course, along the edges of the desk, the windowsills and a couple of other places rested that nasty, granular black fingerprint powder which the crime scene folks never seem to clean up.

I didn't want to sit down on the couch, on the off chance that the cops would come back for some sort of follow up. Instead, I stood there at the door, took in the view, and contemplated my next move.

With it being winter, I had a pair of gloves in my jacket pocket. If I wanted to, I'd be able to rifle through the various cabinets, along with the desk drawers, but what would I be looking for? In the dead man's office, what sort of clue would I find to point to someone other than Thayer as the killer?

Maybe I was overthinking things. Maybe if I just sat down on the couch and waited long enough, some clue would poke its head out of one of the corners and catch my attention. Who knew? Maybe Colonel Mustard had left some tobacco specks behind, and if I spotted them I could wrap the whole thing up today, free my client's husband and be acclaimed as a detecting genius.

If I were lucky, I'd find a candlestick with the colonel's fingerprints on it.

Or, more likely, I'd just find a bunch of dry, academic stuff that wouldn't make a whole lot of sense to an untutored jock like me.

I cracked the door open to make sure Felicia was still out, saw no one else moving around out there, and shut the door again to begin searching.

At the end of about half an hour, I was seriously thinking about giving up the private detective stuff and going back to running The Blaster as my sole occupation. I'd come across lots of files with old student exams and papers; quite a few haphazard notes, most of which seemed to be the starting points for books and articles Hartness would now never get around to writing; and clips of pages torn out of textbooks with all sorts of scrawling on them.

No passionate love letters from old girl friends, no demands for blackmail money, no threatening missives about what a low-down, dirty so-and-so Hartness was.

In fact, I hadn't found anything of a really personal nature at all. In and of itself not conclusive of anything, as most material like that, if it existed, would be at the man's house or apartment. Still, would have been nice to find some indication of nefarious actions on the man's part, something that could at least point to motive for someone else.

Of course, I'd spent all my time on the cabinets and files, constantly circling what could very well be the single biggest source of information in the office, the computer on Hartness's desk.

As with the actual physical office, I counted it as a decent possibility that the cops hadn't spent much time going through the deceased prof's computer. The very fact that it still sat on his desk indicated as much. If the attack and murder had been a true mystery to them, they no doubt would have scoured the darned thing. As it was, glomming onto Thayer practically as soon as they arrived on scene, why would they have bothered?

I decided to bother.

As I sat down at the desk, I paused to ponder whether I was about to do something brilliant or moronic. On the one hand, I could potentially stumble across something that would really break the case. Then again, even with Felix Thayer in the bullseye the case was still officially considered open until a conviction, or lack thereof. Ergo, one could view my actions as tampering with evidence.

If so, the state licensing board would probably yank my P.I. paper quicker than I could throw my hands up to ask for mercy.

As I was about to start punching buttons and see what I could pull up, a third possible avenue presented itself to me. If I managed to get official police permission to examine the darned thing, I'd be in the clear all around.

And as luck would have it, I just happened to know someone who was high enough up the chain to give me said permission.

Pleased as possible with myself at my sudden brainstorm, I got up from the desk, took a look around to make sure everything was in the exact spot it had been when I walked in, cracked the door open to determine that a) Felicia hadn't made it back yet and b) no one else was in the outer area of the suite, and strolled out, acting every inch as if I belonged there.

Yep, I was pretty tickled with myself.

Now all I had to do was convince a guy, who from all indications absolutely hated my guts, to let me snag the prof's computer.

CHAPTER FOURTEEN

WITH THE COAST STILL CLEAR, I decided to push my luck by edging my way into Thayer's office as well. Although clearly as much the crime scene as the victim's, I was on slightly firmer ground here. My employment by Susan Thayer gave me a justifiable excuse for at least believing it was okay to be in her husband's place, even though legally that wouldn't hold up much if the cops decided to make a fuss about it.

At first, Thayer's office appeared a carbon copy of his colleague's. Same metal cabinets, same type desk, even positioned in pretty much the same way. His computer, though of a newer-looking model, occupied about the same position as the one on Hartness' s desk.

Thayer's machine didn't hold as much attraction for me. As the chief suspect, I pretty much assumed all of his effects would have been gone over with a meticulous thoroughness. And obviously, any of the incriminating stuff, the supposed murder weapon, the bloody clothes, or anything else, would already be downtown in the custody of the DA's office.

I considered calling Daniel Lancaster to see if he could get me a look at the evidence list, provided the DA had turned it over to the defense, but dismissed it almost at once. That kind of thinking was the sort of straw grasping one would only do if there were no other avenues available.

I made a mental note to ask Susan Thayer if the cops had taken any of her husband's personal effects from their home. Providence isn't the largest city in Missouri, but no one should mistake our police force for a bunch of Barney Fifes. The cops were damned good at their jobs, the detectives especially, and even with a slam dunk case I had no doubt that Nichols and his folks had gone the extra mile, left no stone unturned, or exceeded any other metaphor one could think of.

Even so, the idea that Thayer had been stupid enough to dump both the weapon and his stained clothing in his office and just wait for the police to show up didn't sit right. The guy was arrogant as all get out, and I would have placed him at the bottom of any list of people I wanted to invite over to my next party, but no matter what you could say about him, he wasn't stupid.

The more I thought about it, the more I leaned towards the theory that he'd been set up. The question to answer, though, was had the set-upper had been after only Hartness, only Thayer or gunning for both men together.

Unfortunately, staring at the prof's empty office wasn't getting me anywhere close to an answer.

I eased the door open and saw that Felicia had returned to her desk. From Thayer's doorway, I couldn't quite make out the rest of the suite, so I brushed my knuckles lightly against the door panel.

Felicia looked back at me, grinned, and gave a slight nod, which I took as indication the rest of the area was empty. I skedaddled out as quickly as I could, on the off chance someone would take that exact split second to walk in and wonder why a big, burly guy was coming out of a professor's office.

No such person, materialized, however, and a few seconds later I was leaning against Felicia's counter, the two of us whispering like conspirators.

Which, I guess, we were.

"Find anything?" she asked.

"Nothing but more questions. Would you happen to know if the cops took anything out of Dr. Thayer's office?"

"You kidding?" An incredulous look stretched across her face. "You think they let any of us staff people anywhere around here while they were doing their investigating stuff? We were all on the outside looking in, with everyone else on campus convinced we had the lowdown and mad we wouldn't share it with them."

"How long did they have you all locked out?" I asked.

Felicia paused and crossed her eyes while she thought about it. "Remember, dude, they found the body on a Friday, and I guess arrested Dr. Thayer the same day. Means they had the weekend to do whatever they needed to. Things have been unlocked and back to normal since last Monday."

"And any hints at all about what they found or didn't find?"

"Uh uh. Like I told you, they kept it close to the vest. The first couple of hours, right after the body had been found, you could tell just by looking at their faces that it was a bad scene in there."

I couldn't help but grin at her.

"What?" she snapped.

"Bad scene," I said. "You sound kind of like a holdover from the seventies."

"Of course. Best R & B ever came from that decade."

"And you don't listen to anything else, right?" I asked.

She gave me that smile again, the one that damned near blew you away if you stood too close.

"Damned straight, dude. Sorry I can't help you more, but if you want to know if they took anything out of those two's offices, you're going to have to ask the cops themselves."

"Yeah," I said. "That's what I'm afraid of."

CHAPTER FIFTEEN

It took some doing, but I managed to track Dr. Marsha Lawrence down in the middle of her morning workout at a local health club. Walking inside, I knew that had Lisa Nolan been with me, she would have probably fainted at the look of the place. It was everything she dreamed The Blaster could be.

With a, for me, tacky color scheme of bright orange and pale green, the place sparkled with an array of dozens, if not hundreds of rowing machines, weight machines, stationary bikes, treadmills, and every other device conceived to help people get in shape. Signs along the front wall pointed to a variety of other areas that included spas, whirlpools, massage rooms and even a steam room.

At ten thirty in the morning in the middle of the week, there was something like two hundred people in there, most of them looking between thirty and fifty and barely breaking a sweat as they had their various machines and weights set to the lowest levels possible.

Yep, Lisa would have been in heaven. Just the thought of all those people making absolutely no progress, which means they'd be shelling out money for a long time to see any results, would have made her beyond giddy.

Inside the front entrance, I looked around but couldn't spot anyone who resembled a middle-aged professor. My time running my own gym, plus my investigative work, has made me pretty good at judging people's professions and lifestyles by evaluating them, but that ability failed me now.

Not wanting to arouse suspicion by wandering around the place bothering all the women clients, I headed over to the customer service counter situated in the middle of the large front area.

The girl behind the counter, a perky blonde wearing an actual, honest to God ponytail, smiled up at me, blue eyes glinting.

"Yes, sir?"

"I'm trying to locate Dr. Marsha Lawrence. Could you point her out please?"

The blue eyes suddenly weren't glinting quite as much. "I'm not sure, I should . . ."

"Nothing like that." I gave her one of my patented smiles. Not one of the ones I'd used back in the wrestling ring, but the one I used when I'd be at a bar after a show and was trying to coax some female fan into having a drink with me. "I work for her accounting firm and have some papers she needs to sign ASAP."

She gave me a look, as if to say she'd never seen an accountant wearing jeans and a leather coat, especially during a weekday.

"You don't look like an accountant," she said.

"It's my day off, but this came up out of the blue and I've got to get her signature. If we don't wrap this deal up today, she's going to lose out on a lot of money."

"Couldn't they just be faxed to her?"

This one could have given even Lisa a few pointers on not falling for a smooth story.

"Well, actually," I said, "they have to be notarized, and I'm a notary. They're also time sensitive, and for some reason Dr. Lawrence isn't answering her phone."

Relenting, the girl pointed to the right and slightly behind her. "You'll probably find her in the yoga room, then. But don't bother her too long, okay?"

I thanked the young woman, turned in the direction indicated, and headed off. Didn't take long to get to the yoga room, but once inside I stopped, looked around, then stepped back out again.

I checked to make sure I was in the right place. Sure enough, an orange and green sign indicated that I was standing next to the yoga room. I glanced back in but still didn't see any frumpy, SJW type professor lady practicing her downward dog.

In fact, there was only one person in the room at the time, and no way could she be the object of my search. Around five seven, though kind of hard to tell with her body tangled like a pretzel, the young woman nicely filled out a form-fitting black leotard. She had thick black hair that she'd bunched behind her head with a pin, and when she glanced up at my intrusion a pair of the darkest, deepest eyes I'd ever seen.

If I'd been about twenty years younger, I'd have had to restrain myself from prancing around the room.

"Looking for someone?" she asked, her voice even and in no way showing the strain of balancing on her hands while slowly rotating her body to the side. The definition I could see in her slim arms, even from across the room, went a long way towards explaining her ease of breath.

"Yeah, sorry," I said, "but the young woman out front told me I'd find Marsha Lawrence in here. You have any idea where she is?"

The brunette unwound herself from her position, stood up and walked over to grab a towel from the side of the mat. "I'm Dr. Lawrence," she said, "what can I do for you?"

I didn't exactly let my mouth hang open from surprise, but I came pretty close. One or two more incidents like that and I'll start agreeing with Lisa Nolan when she tells me how much of a throwback I am.

I introduced myself, explained why I wanted to talk to her and immediately saw the barriers start to raise.

"You're working for Felix?" she asked.

"Well, technically I guess you could say I'm working for his wife, but it more or less amounts to the same thing."

"Then I really don't think I want to talk to you."

"Why's that?"

She took a final swipe of her face with the towel, then placed it inside a black gym bag lying off to the side. Standing up, she turned and faced me directly for the first time since I'd entered the room.

"Because I don't particularly feel like helping the man who killed my colleague."

"Dr. Thayer's your colleague as well," I pointed out, hoping she wouldn't take a swing at me.

"Yes, but Michael Hartness was at least a decent human being."

"And Felix Thayer isn't?"

She slipped into a pair of soft-soled shoes and slung the bag around her shoulder. "Felix Thayer is about as far from decent as a man can get, and if you're working for him I'd have serious doubts about your standards."

"Are you talking as an academic, a liberal, or as a woman?" I asked.

Now she began to flat out glare at me. "Because I work at the university, you automatically assume I'm a liberal? I'll have you know I voted for Bush. Three times, if you include Jeb."

"Well," I said, "there is the whole sociology professor thing. What would you assume if our positions were reversed?"

She continued glaring, but only for a few seconds before she softened up. Another heartbeat or two, and she began to chuckle, then flat out laugh.

"No doubt I'd assume the same thing you did," she said. "I guess I can't blame you."

"No," I said, "but there is a way you could make up for falsely accusing me of prejudice."

"And what would that be? By the way, from where I stand I didn't falsely accuse you. You were prejudicing me. I merely said I'd have done the same in your position."

"Point taken," I said. "How about having a cup of coffee with me? We can iron all this out and never falsely assume each other again."

Her smile eased off, though the laughter was still there under the surface. "I still don't like the idea of speaking with anyone working for Felix. Or his wife."

"Then how about that cup of coffee and I'll just listen while you talk. That way, you're only speaking to me, not with me."

She shook her head but held out her hand. "Let's try this again. Dr. Marsha Lawrence."

"Sam Quinton," I said, taking her hand. "Private investigator."

She now took a step back and gave me a full once over. "I must say you have the build for it. You work out much?"

Now it was my turn to chuckle, though I doubt my attempt was as sexy as hers. "I own a gym, which lets me use the equipment whenever I want."

"Nice."

"Plus I used to be a pro wrestler."

The smile, which I kind of liked, came back again. "A wrestler who turns into a private eye? That sounds like a hell of a story."

"I'll tell you mine if you tell me yours," I said, noting to myself that this week was probably a record for me. Two attractive women, both about my age, within the course of a couple of days.

CHAPTER SIXTEEN

"HE'S A CREEP. A one-hundred percent, unadulterated creep."

"Don't hide behind all that academic jargon, doc. Tell how you really feel about him."

Marsha Lawrence and I were sitting in a corner table at one of the downtown coffee shops that pop up with an almost regular precision throughout Providence. Outside of Seattle, you probably won't find any community in the nation with as many coffee shops per capita as our little university town, most of them situated in the downtown area within walking distance of the campus.

We'd managed to arrive during the sweet spot right after the morning rush and about half an hour before the lunch crowd showed up. Meaning the noise level was down to a tolerable level and we could hear each other talk without bellowing.

"How do you get more plain spoken than unadulterated creep?" Dr. Lawrence asked.

"Okay. I guess you've got a point there. Let me put it this way. Can you be more specific as to the degrees of his creepiness?"

"The degrees? Since you tracked me down, I assume you've been to my office, correct?"

I nodded as I took a sip of my plain black.

"And you no doubt talked to Felicia, right? It's okay if you did. I'm sure she was as discreet as possible."

I gave the most non-committal head movement possible. "The creepiness?" I repeated.

She took a sip of her drink, some sort of sugared-up thing with an Italian sounding name, before answering. "He made a pass at me once."

"At the university?"

"In my office, believe it or not. Came in to discuss some budgetary figures for the department, and next thing I knew he was ogling me up and down and damned near salivating."

"That the extent of it?"

She smiled. "If it was, would I call it a pass? He took hold of my hand and started stroking my forearm, telling me how beautiful I looked, how sitting next to me during department meetings drove him nuts."

"At least the man has taste," I said, which drew another smile from her. "I assume you reported him to the university's higher ups?"

"Not hardly."

I frowned. "Really? In this progressive day and age? Isn't filing a complaint of some kind the automatic thing to do? Or was this a while ago?"

"It was last year. And I handled it in a more direct way."

I felt as if I were being setup for a punch line. "Which was?"

Now the smile came full wattage. "I smacked him with a solid right cross. Lifted him right out of his chair and onto the floor."

It was my turn to grin. "I noticed your muscle tone while you were finishing up your yoga."

"Damned straight, bubba. Like I said, I like to think I'm not one of your shrinking violet academic types. He had a hell of a time for about a week explaining the bruise on his face."

"Nice," I said. "Be interesting to find out how he explained it to his wife."

Professor Lawrence snorted. "Be my guess it wasn't the first time he had to explain weird stuff to her."

"You know," I said. "I'm starting to wonder if I'm going to find anyone with a nice thing to say about the man."

"If you do, I can pretty much guarantee it won't be anyone around campus."

"Was the one time the extent of his creepiness?" I asked.

"To me? Yes. After that first time, he learned his lesson. But to others of the staff? Especially anyone he considered beneath him? Lord, the day isn't long enough to list all of his crap."

"And I'm guessing he thought everyone else was beneath him?" I asked.

"Don't bother using the past tense, buster. I guarantee you right about now he's wherever he is pondering how awesome he is compared to all other mortals."

"Where he is, is sitting in a cell down at the Carson County jail," I pointed out.

"So? You think that stops him from thinking how wonderful he is, then you don't know Felix Thayer. And if you get him off, you'll just be confirming his self-image."

I spread my hands. "Hey, I'm just gathering information."

"How about gathering this. Felix Thayer is the kind of man who would kick an old lady down in the street, then turn around and sue her for dulling the polish on his shoes. And after he took said old lady for everything she had, he'd probably get it on with her granddaughter just to show what a stud he is. This the kind of person you want to earn a living off of?"

"Actually, it's only part of a living," I said. "This is just one of my gigs."

"Oh? What else do you do? Process serve on single mothers trying to keep a roof over their heads?"

I could now see the sociology professor coming out in her. I'd liked her a whole lot more the other way.

"I own a gym," I said. "The Blaster?"

The lady prof arched an eyebrow at me. "Really? That's your place? I always heard it was owned by some broken-down, stumblebum ex wrestler."

"Guilty," I said.

She pursed her lips and knitted her brows. "Let me get this straight. You were a wrestler and now you own a health club?"

"Gym," I corrected her.

"Gym. But you're also a detective? How exactly does that happen?"

"Long story," I said. "But right now, I'm focused more on your co-worker. Anyone around campus like him?"

Dr. Lawrence laughed. "Not that I ever heard of. Seriously, the man was an absolute pig. He even bullied the staff people. Not just the secretaries. The custodial staff. Everybody who was lower or lesser than him."

I skulled that one over for a moment as she continued drinking her coffee.

"Anyone in particular?" I asked after a few minutes.

She put her cup down and gave it some thought. "No one in particular, although lately he did seem to kind of have it in for George."

"Who's George?"

"One of the nighttime staff. A sweet kid."

"How young of a kid?"

"George?" She gave it some thought. "I don't know. Somewhere in his twenties, maybe early thirties."

"How long's he been on the job?" I asked.

Dr. Lawrence shrugged. "He's been in our building for about a year now. But working for the university?" Another shrug. "Who knows?"

"Last name?" I asked.

Another long pause as those brows knitted and her eyes focused. "Don't know if I've ever heard his last name. He's just George."

"George the janitor," I said.

"That's right."

"You say he works mainly nights?" I asked.

"Yep."

"Would he have had all that much interaction with Thayer? Enough to get on the guy's bad side?"

Her eyes lit up as she grinned. "You haven't spent all that much time around teachers, have you?"

"Not since I barely graduated high school."

"That's what I thought. It's like this. We don't have set hours or anything. Besides our class time, we come and go pretty much as we please."

"Aren't you guys supposed to be in your offices though, in case students come around?"

"Sure. For all of about three hours a week. Other than that, our time's pretty much our own."

"You saying Thayer spent a lot of time in the office at night?"

"I'm saying he was in and out all of the time."

"What about Hartness?"

"Same thing. Though they did the best they could to avoid each other."

"Why's that?" I asked.

She paused, her cup halfway to her lips. I gave it a heartbeat or two as she thought through her hesitation.

She put the cup down and focused squarely on me.

"I've got to be careful how I'm talking here," she said.

"Okay," I said. I was getting kind of used to that attitude.

"I don't want to unfairly impugn a colleague."

"Which colleague would that be? Way I see it, one of them's already been impugned about as much as he can be."

Dr. Lawrence didn't lose the seriousness in her eyes, but she did quirk a smile at me. "I wasn't testing you with big words," she said.

"No problem. I managed to figure it out from the context. Which colleague?"

"Actually, it's both of them. I don't feel all that comfortable discussing office politics with someone I just met, working for Felix or no."

"But there is something there," I said. "Something that could be at the bottom of all this."

"Possibly. Though it may just be a matter of attaching a lot more seriousness to something than actually exists."

"And you don't want to say what it is?"

She shook her head. "I just wouldn't feel comfortable."

We talked on for a little while longer, but there wasn't much more she would give me. We swapped phone numbers in case she had a change of mind, and after I settled the tab we went our separate ways.

As I walked to my car, I mentally reviewed my to do list and added one more thing to it.

It looked like somewhere down the line I had to talk with a certain janitor.

CHAPTER SEVENTEEN

DR. KURT SCHUMACHER WAS NEXT ON THE LIST. It took some doing, but later that day I managed to track him down at one of the university's seven libraries.

Felicia hadn't told me much about the man, but the little bit she had said had pretty much prepared me for what I'd find. "Low person on the totem pole" she'd said, which led me to expect a fairly youngish man, serious-looking as all hell, who still put a hundred percent into his teaching duties.

When I walked into the library, which had only one floor, thus making it one of the smaller ones on campus, the place looked particularly dead. A couple of workers halfheartedly shuffled papers at a side counter; a scattered handful of young people I presumed to be students slumped into easy chairs and listening to earbuds while they stared at tablets; and off in the corner one serious-looking guy crouched over a couple of honest-to-God books.

Bingo.

I made my way over to the man, sitting at a table with a mound of books, loose papers and, of course, a small laptop open in front of him. I stopped a couple of feet away.

He was focused on whatever he was working on, poring over the laptop screen, then glancing at one of the books before scribbling something down on a yellow legal tablet. It looked to me as if he'd been absorbed in the project for hours.

I stood there a few minutes before finally realizing that his work had him so consumed he wasn't aware of anything around him. Taking a card from my wallet, I made my way to his table.

I had to stand just to the side of him for nearly a minute before he raised his head up, glanced at me, and frowned.

"Dr. Schumacher?" I asked.

"Yes?" He looked me over warily as I handed him my card.

He glanced at it, frowned again, then handed it back. "Really? A private eye?"

"It's what the card says. May I sit down?"

He gave me a searching examination before gesturing toward the other seat at his table. As I pulled the chair out, I saw a thick, blue book resting on it. Sheepishly, Schumacher reached over and removed it.

"Sorry," he said. "I've been at this article for quite a while, and things are starting to sprawl on me."

I smiled, hoping to put the guy at ease. "No problem."

"Can I assume you're here about Dr. Thayer?" he asked.

"What makes you think that?"

Dr. Schumacher put out the smallest of smiles and shook his head. "I have no divorce pending, no payments of any consequence that I'm behind on, and no criminal matters currently outstanding against me, at least that I know of. Ergo," he spread his hands out, "I'm guessing you're here about Felix."

"Good guess," I said.

"To help or hinder?"

"To find out the truth."

Schumacher closed an open book and rearranged some of his materials, no doubt giving himself time to think. "You mean in this day and age someone actually wants to know the truth?"

"One or two of us still around."

"Including?"

"His wife."

"Aww, Susan."

I nodded. "Know her well?"

He shrugged, and his blue eyes blinked. "Met her a couple of times. Faculty parties and such. I think I may have only spoken a grand total of about thirty words to her all told. Seems nice enough from what I've seen."

"But you and Dr. Thayer are co-workers, right?"

Schumacher nodded. "But that doesn't mean that we spend a lot of time socializing. Even though we're around people all the time, teaching, especially at the university level, can be a rather lonely occupation."

"How long have you been in your job?"

The eyes blinked a couple more times. "How could that possibly be relevant? Are you investigating me in some way?"

"Not at all," I said. "I'm just out scooping up as much information as I can."

He peered at me and shuffled his hands a bit on the table. "What exactly did Mrs. Thayer hire you for? From what they say on the news, plus the unofficial grapevine, it's pretty much an open and shut case. I would think that the Thayers's money would be put to better use on the courtroom side of things."

"Meaning you think he's guilty?"

For a second there, Schumacher looked at me as if I'd started talking backwards. "Don't you? They seem to have a pretty convincing case. Hard to argue with all of that physical evidence."

"I hear that Thayer's pretty smart."

Schumacher frowned at me, almost as if I'd passed gas. "Calling Felix Thayer 'pretty smart' is about the wildest understatement I've ever heard. The man's a leading light in our field."

Now it was my turn to peer at the man. "You know, you're about the first person I've run into who's spoken favorably of him."

Schumacher squirmed, and he looked down at the papers in front of him. "All I can tell you is he's been quite a help to me. Really showed me the ropes my first few years here."

"Where you from originally?" I asked.

Now came the peering again. "I really don't see how that's any of your business, sir."

"Look, doc. I'm not trying to steal your identity or anything. I'm trying to dig up as much as I can about Dr. Thayer in order to figure out what's going on, and I need context for whatever information I get."

"Which presupposes I'm going to provide you with said information."

No wonder this guy had a couple of initials after his name. He was sharp.

"I'm not out to blow up any land mines, doc. Just trying to get a feel for the man."

"In that case," Schumacher leaned back in his chair, "I've been at the college for three years now, and Dr. Thayer has been my unofficial mentor for almost that long."

"What's an unofficial mentor do?"

"Helped me get acclimated around, complete open-door policy whenever something comes up. Even helped me place a couple of my early articles in prestigious journals. You know, the old publish or perish conundrum."

I stared at Schumacher for a moment. The blue eyes stared back with no hint of concern.

"Some folks have said he was kind of hard to be around."

The gaze flicked down to the papers again and held there for a longer period before he made eye contact with me again.

"As I said, I've had no problems with him at all. He's been a great help to me."

"I hear he had a habit of stealing colleague's work. How much 'help' did he give you with those articles?"

Schumacher flinched, and a hint of red crept into his face. "He did a couple of light edits, pointed out a few things I hadn't considered. But it was my work."

"I have no doubt of that, professor. But tell me this. Did Thayer's name end up on those articles along with yours?"

The red became more pronounced now, and he picked up a pen and clasped it so tightly I wondered it didn't break.

"It was a matter of professional courtesy, that's all. He assisted me, so of course I gave him credit."

I thought of pushing it more, but Schumacher's body language, much more than his words, told me everything I really needed.

"How about other people?" I asked. "Any issues there?"

"What sort of other people?"

"Oh, you know," I said, "what about students?"

Schumacher grimaced and slumped a bit in his chair. He fiddled with the pen for a few seconds before looking back up at me. "I'd rather not talk about anything like that, if you don't mind."

"Dr. Schumacher, if you know something—" I began.

"Does it really matter? After all, if he killed Michael what's the difference whether—"

"I thought you were the one just telling me what a great guy Thayer is. Are you already convinced he's guilty?"

Another few seconds of mumbling and fumbling before Schumacher looked up at me. "I really have to get back to work, okay? Honestly, there's nothing more I can tell you about any of this."

I suddenly felt like a pud for hassling a guy who was just trying to get by within the system. And really, would any more hard info tell me something I didn't already strongly suspect? Namely, that the good Dr. Felix Thayer was an A Number One first class prick?

"Okay," I said.

I got up, thanked him, buttoned up my coat and headed out into the Missouri winter.

As I was leaving, I stood on the steps of the library and pulled out my phone. I didn't have a call, didn't need to make one, but I wanted a reason to be standing in place that wouldn't look suspicious.

A tan Nissan was parked about half a block away, the engine idling, and I could make out two heads in the front seat.

I wasn't positive, but I had a strong feeling that I'd seen that same car a couple of other times earlier in the day.

CHAPTER EIGHTEEN

I HAD A CHOICE TO MAKE. I could go on to the next name on my list, interviewing people and learning everything I could about Felix Thayer, or I could pull some sort of cowboy stunt and see if there was something going on with the Nissan, though I had a pretty good idea what the story was there.

After skulling it over for a few minutes, I threw my Cherokee into gear and pulled out of the parking space, one eye on the road ahead and one on the rearview mirror.

When I got to the stop sign that would take me off campus and into the normal flow of traffic, I began to turn right, and sure enough, about six spaces behind me the Nissan did the same.

Confrontation time or play the long game?

I decided to let it lie for a while, keep an eye on my backside, and let things run their course.

Pulling into a grocery store parking lot, I put the car in park and pulled out my phone. I noticed the Nissan drive right on by, seemingly without a care in the world. It only took a couple of phone calls, and promising a few favors down the road, before I had Dr. Harold Shipton's address.

As I headed out again, I looked all around but couldn't see the Nissan anywhere.

Dr. Shipton lived in a fairly nice subdivision on the south side of town, and as I pulled up outside the brick-fronted, two story home with a wide porch that ran almost the length of the yard, I considered, not for the first time in the last several years, that I may have picked the wrong line of work. His place wasn't super extravagant or anything, but it sure beat my two-bedroom apartment.

The few phone calls I'd made, plus Felicia's info, had netted the information that Dr. Shipton, a full professor, brought in somewhere in the low six figures a year. A nice income if you can get it, but it wouldn't really account for the home he seemed able to afford.

On the other hand, I'd also unearthed that Shipton had been unmarried and childless his entire life, which by itself could raise his standard of living quite a bit.

Walking up to the front porch and ringing the bell, I was greeted by a large, ominous barking from inside, somewhere just the other side of the door. After about half a minute of that came a scraping sound, and a second later the door opened up.

"Dr. Shipton?" I asked in my most pleasant manner. I didn't know what sort of beast he had on the other side of that door, but I wanted to present myself as the least amount of threat I possibly could.

"Yes? What can I do for you?"

He was a compactly built man standing around five eight or so, and I pegged his age at early to mid-fifties. Dressed in chinos and a light blue polo shirt, he didn't come off as particularly muscular, though I couldn't see any signs of fat on him either. He had a thick mass of silver hair, light gray eyes and a nose that showed a few reddened, broken capillaries.

I also got the faintest whiff of gin coming from him.

Early afternoon, and a school day no less.

I introduced myself, showing my wallet with license photostat. He didn't seem all that impressed.

"Like I said, what do you need?"

"I'd like to talk to you about Felix Thayer."

He frowned even harder, his eyes narrowing to slits. "Why me? And what exactly is this about?"

"I've been hired by his wife to investigate his recent—troubles. I'm talking to everyone who works with him. Trying to get a complete picture." I smiled, hoping to put the man at ease.

The gray eyes narrowed even more. "What you mean is that you're going around making a damned nuisance of yourself."

I took a deep breath, reminding myself that antagonizing a possible witness wouldn't help get me anywhere, and definitely wouldn't help Thayer if in fact he was innocent. Even so, I felt an overwhelming urge to view Shipton as a heavy bag and work out for a few minutes.

"Could we talk inside, Dr. Shipton? It is kind of cold out here."

"You want a complete picture of Felix Thayer, mister? Fine, I'll give you one. He's the most arrogant, obnoxious, weasely person I've ever had the pleasure of sharing an office with. If he didn't kill Dr. Hartness, he probably would have if he'd gotten half a chance. Far as I'm concerned, do the world a favor and just send him off to the chair already."

The heavy bag motif sharpened in my mind. I shook my head to dispel the image and went with a gut instinct. "What'd Thayer do?" I asked. "Walk off with an award you expected to get or something?"

Shipton snorted. "An award? Young man, I've been in my profession nearly thirty-five years. I've received more awards than I know what to do with. There was nothing that Felix could say or do to get to me."

"But you don't seem to like him very much."

A soft bark came from inside and to the right, and Shipton turned his head in that direction. "It's okay, Baxter," he said before stepping out onto the porch and shutting the door.

"Don't read anything into my opinions, Mr. Quinton," he said, his voice softening a bit. "I'm an old, ready-to-retire academic who managed to make it to full professor. You know what that means?"

"The way I understand, it means you can do pretty much whatever you want," I said.

"That's only one side. The other side is that I don't have to worry a whole lot about what other people do or say. It may seem like a contradiction in terms, but by the time you get to my level, ordinary university politics don't really affect you a whole lot."

"Okay."

"You may want to look into what was going on inside the department. See if there were any animosity specifically between those two men."

"It's obvious they didn't get along," I said.

"True, to a point." Shipton's face split into a huge, beaming smile. "But why didn't they get along? What was it that came between them?"

"Meaning what?"

"That's for you to find out," Shipton said. "But just because I don't worry about politics anymore, doesn't mean that's true for everyone."

CHAPTER NINETEEN

"WHAT MAKES YOU THINK HARTNESS HAD A COMPUTER?" Lt. William Santiago asked me, his mouth curling in a bit of a sneer.

"Besides the fact that it's the twenty-first century, and it stands to reason everyone has a computer in their office?"

We were sitting in the lieutenant's office. Santiago, a recent transplant to Providence from the Chicago police department, was somewhere in his forties. Even so, at five ten he was lean and muscled with little sign of fat. Made even more obvious by the fact that, on a police lieutenant's salary, he somehow managed to wear tailored suits every day.

Today, he had on a dark brown wool suit with eggshell shirt that went well with his thick, brown hair and eyes.

If only the guy would smile at me now and then, he'd be great.

"What I meant," Santiago said in a slow, careful enunciation, "is that maybe he used a tablet or pad, even a laptop. Why would you automatically assume he had a computer in his office?"

He glared at me as he spoke, almost daring me to 'fess up that I'd already seen the inside of said office.

I gave him the blankest look I could muster. "Just stands to reason, lieutenant. Sure, he may have had all sorts of devices at home and stuff, but I'd say a regular desktop is probably standard issue across the university."

"Uh huh," Santiago said. "And of course, assuming it's such

standard issue, you must also logically assume that us dumb cops didn't think to check it out."

"Why would you? You had no reason to do so. Within, what, about ten minutes you'd tracked down the guy's killer. What would be the point of wasting manpower to check out other avenues? You had Thayer, almost literally red handed, so why bother that much with sidelines?"

"But you don't think we've got the right guy, is that it? And in your zeal for justice you're wanting to go through the dead man's stuff."

I smiled, giving him the "aw shucks" grin from back in my ring days. The "aw shucks," one of my patented expressions, basically said let's all be friends and get along. It was the kind of look I'd give a fellow performer, to show no hard feelings, right before I kneed him in the groin.

Santiago gave me nothing but a cold stare in return.

The older I get, the less the "aw shucks" seems to work.

Or maybe Santiago didn't know what it meant to have friends.

"Word is that you had a dustup with Sean O'Flaherty the other day," he said.

"Word gets around doesn't it, Lieutenant. I'm assuming this word came from one Josh Nichols."

"The sergeant did mention something about it, yes."

"Probably concerned for my safety," I said. "Doesn't want to see anything happen to one of his nearest and dearest friends."

"Actually, I got the impression it was more along the lines of we've been overworked lately as it is and he didn't want another murder case to land on his desk."

"Sure," I said, "could be that."

"On the other hand," Santiago continued, "O'Flaherty's been kind of a pain in the ass ever since he showed up here, and we wouldn't mind a chance to run him in."

"Any possibility you could do it for less than taking me completely out of the game?"

Santiago leaned back and folded his arms across his chest. "You know, Quinton, despite your punk attitude, I get the idea you're a halfway competent investigator."

"Mind if I quote you on my business cards?"

"Yes, I do mind. Even so, you really think there's some connection between Sean O'Flaherty and the Hartness murder?"

I sat up straighter in my chair. "I hadn't been on the case half a day before Sean and his bully boys came around to see me."

"Working on anything else at the moment?"

"Nothing but a couple of low-rent skip traces. And those are on hold until something breaks. So no, nothing that would be worth Sean's time or effort. Besides, he specifically referenced the Thayer deal when he tried to buy me off."

Santiago drummed his fingers on his desk for a minute. "We didn't bother going over Hartness's computer," he finally said. "Didn't seem worth the effort since we had your client sewed up inside of an hour."

"Did it strike you at all odd that you could grab the guy that quick?" I asked. "After all, he's supposed to be kind of smart, yet he left a trail a mile long."

"You spend much time around these university types?"

I shrugged. "Now and then. In this town, it's kind of hard to avoid them."

"So you probably know that Ph.D. isn't exactly a synonym for being smart."

"I've heard that. You're saying that Thayer may be book smart but not so much in common sense," I said.

"You've met him already, I assume?"

"I have."

"And?"

"I'd probably agree with your assessment. Still doesn't make him a murderer."

"He's also a prick," Santiago said with the merest hint of a smile.

"He is that."

"Edges him closer to the murderer category."

"Maybe, but think about it Lieutenant. Is even the dumbest guy out there going to brain his co-worker, walk six feet to his own office, then deposit both the bloody weapon and bloody clothes right where you can find them?"

"It's what we in law enforcement call an open and shut case. Happens all the time," Santiago replied.

"Depends on how you look at it."

"The suits upstairs like open and shut cases. For that matter, so do certain civic leaders."

"Including a particular university chancellor?" I asked.

Santiago spread his hands. "We already determined that Thayer's pretty much a prick."

"Means including the chancellor. What about Providence's resident Irish godfather?"

Santiago drummed his fingers again. His nails looked manicured. What sort of hardass Chicago cop manicures his nails?

"Yeah," he finally said. "I got to admit that when Nichols filled me in on that it got me wondering."

"Wondering enough to let me get a crack at Michael Hartness's computer?"

"Compromise," Santiago said.

"Shoot."

"Wondering enough that we'll look at it, and I'll let you know if we find anything germane to your client."

I briefly considered pushing it, then decided I'd already gotten more than I could reasonably expect.

"What about your superiors and the civic leaders?" I asked.

"I've left jobs before," Santiago said.

CHAPTER TWENTY

I PICKED UP THE TAIL ABOUT A block away from the station. Just about to turn into the parking garage where I'd stored my car, daytime street parking in Providence being only slightly more scarce than New York, I turned a hair to my right and saw the two men coming my way.

As soon as I turned, both of them stopped right there on the sidewalk and began talking to each other, their faces turned from me.

Uh huh.

If they were Sean O'Flaherty's guys, things were even tougher for the local mob than I'd thought. If they belonged to someone else, or were just two muggers straight out of the 1970's who'd only just now awakened into a new world, they were still about as out of place as possible.

Both men looked to be in their mid-twenties, though with the bulky coats and stocking caps they wore, it was hard to get a good read on their features. I did see enough to know that one was black and the other Hispanic of some sort, and they looked big enough to get the job done most of the time.

Again, though, the dark-colored pea coats they were wearing made determining their exact physiques a little difficult.

Both of them stood around five eleven, a bit shorter than me, and as far as I could see were smooth-shaven, though the black looked like he was attempting to grow a rather sickly goatee.

Wonderful, I thought.

I considered turning in place and heading back to the station and throwing myself on Santiago for protection. Then I realized that if word got around what a pushover I'd become a lot of the cops would stop coming around the gym, and Lisa would blame me for our drop in revenue.

I saw no other option but to keep on my way and see what developed with the two yahoos.

What developed was that as I headed into one of the side doors of the parking garage, they immediately stopped talking to each other and came right in after me. I knew this because as soon as I'd gotten inside I darted around the nearest corner and shucked off my coat.

Not so much to use the old Blond Bomber muscles to inspire terror into them as to give me ease of movement.

Like the low-rent hoods I'd already determined they were, they walked inside and fell right into my trap.

"Hi, fellas," I said as they came around the same corner I had.

They stopped, momentarily startled to see their prey waiting for them, and in that moment of suspension I pinned the Hispanic man with a right hook to the jaw.

He spun around once, staggered back up against the cold concrete garage wall and propped himself against the wall.

Damnit. I'd hoped he'd fall flat on the ground and be out of the picture.

In the meantime, of course, his buddy had begun moving in on me, and I now had my side turned to him.

I kept turning, as fast as I could, and got around to facing him just as he reached out with his own hook. But the dude was sloppy, kind of off-center, and I suspected that his pea coat concealed a little more weight than he should own at his age.

A quick side duck on my part, and the black guy's punch sailed right past me, then I was homing back in on him and putting most of my not-inconsiderable weight behind a swift jab into his gut.

The black dude folded over and went to his knees, giving me barely enough time to rip an elbow up and to the side, connecting with the chin of the Hispanic, who by this point had detached himself from the wall and lunged at me again. His jaws snapped together with a crack that almost echoed around the garage, and he went down to join his buddy on the ground.

Looking around, I didn't see anyone around, and I stepped far enough backward that I could keep both of the yutzes within my field of vision as I decided what to do with them.

Having come out of the police station, I naturally didn't have my gun with me. I plucked out my cell phone and began to call either Santiago or Nichols to report a near assault. I paused before I'd punched a single button, though, and considered other options as my two running buddies began groaning and rolling around on the cold concrete floor.

I assumed their presence had something to do with the Thayer case, the natural assumption being that they'd come to me courtesy of Sean O'Flaherty. But while I didn't know much about the local outfit's organization, especially in the wake of Paddy O'Brien's departure, looking at the two low-rents rolling around on the ground I couldn't quite see them working for someone as quietly smooth as O'Flaherty had come off.

Which led me to wonder just who they were working for.

I studied them for a minute as they lay there moaning and groaning. For no particular reason I could pin down, I got the feeling that the black, though he looked a bit tougher, was probably a little more malleable than his partner. It was a close call, though. Six of one and half a dozen of the other, as my mom used to say, as neither of them were exactly what one would call tough guys.

Even so, I picked the black, bent down, and gave the Hispanic guy another poke on the jaw, causing him to collapse senseless again. Glancing to the side, I saw the other one now awake and staring at me. I gave him a scowl I used to use in the wrestling ring to make myself seem fearsome and out of control.

"Sheeit, man," the dude said. "Who the hell you think you're fooling looking like that? Call the cops and have them come pick me up, but don't think I'm gonna tell you nothin.'"

Damn, my fearsome scowl used to scare the heck out of ten-year-olds. Maybe I needed to practice it some more.

Probably didn't quite mesh with the gray starting to show in my hair.

"Why are you following me?" I asked.

The man shook his head, grimacing with the pain as he was still a little woozy. "I know how this works, bubba. The cops come get me and my lawyer steps in. You're nothing official, just a private snoop, which means you can't do shit to me."

"Don't be too sure of that," I said as I came up from my crouch and gave him a kick in the ribs.

"Aaggh!" The hoodlum curled into a fetal position and clutched his mid-section.

"O'Flaherty send you to hassle me?" I asked.

"Who?" the punk groaned.

I lifted my foot as if to kick him again.

"Hey, man, please don't," he cried out. "Who's O'Flaherty?"

"The man who hired you, dumbbell. Your boss. Or don't you know who you're working for?"

"Sure I know who I work for."

"So what did Sean want you to do to me?"

"Who?"

This time, I placed the foot directly on the portion of his ribs I'd kicked before. I didn't press down or anything, just levered enough pressure to make him aware the foot was there. If I was going to break him, I had to do it quick before his buddy started stirring.

"Stop playing games with me, slug. What did O'Flaherty want you to do? Last chance."

He took in a quick sip of air, as if to gather himself. "Don't kick me again, man. But I don't know who you're talking about. We were hired by this guy in a bar. Gave us your picture, told us about where to find you, and said we were to mess you up a bit."

The old "guy in a bar line." It sounded phony as hell, but as I considered the amateurism of these two, I began to doubt they worked for the local mob, no matter how far it had fallen since Paddy's days.

"What'd this guy look like?" I asked.

"I don't know. Just a guy. Came in to Jimmy's place one night. Looking for us. Said he'd heard we were good for some rough stuff now and then and did we want to pick up a little pocket money."

"Did he ask for a money back guarantee if you blew it?" I asked.

"Naw, man. Just said to rough you up a bit so you'd get the message."

"What message?"

"Huh?"

I pressed my foot a little harder. "What message were you supposed to give me?"

"To back off your case. Aww, goddammit, it's hard for me to think when you're doing that."

"Tough. Back off what case?"

"How the hell do I know? We were told to tell you to back off and go back to your barbells, or something like that."

"And this came from O'Flaherty?" I asked, pressing the foot down even harder.

"Aggh! Fuck man, no. I'm telling you, I don't know any O'Flaherty. Now, goddammit, ease up."

I backed off. Either the guy was telling the truth, or he was a hell of a lot tougher than he looked.

Still, it didn't make a lot of sense. And I had to get this over with quick before someone wandered into the garage and called the cops on me

"Let's back up then. Some guy, who you don't know, came into Jimmy's and sought you out."

"That's right. Jackson there and I got kind of a rep around town."

"Must not be much of one," I said. "I'm the one standing over you and I've never heard of you."

He grimaced, but didn't say anything in response.

"Was this stranger a go-between?" I asked.

"Yeah, that's the impression Jackson got. Just someone who'd picked up a couple of bills to pass on the job."

"You get a name from this guy? Name of the person who hired him?"

"Naw, man. That's not how it works. The dude, whoever he is, was after the dental stuff."

I skulled that one around for a moment, wondering if my minor-league felon had begun speaking in tongues, before I got it.

"Deniability?" I asked.

"Yeah, that's it. Deniability. Like in layers, you know?"

His partner began to moan and move a bit, making me figure it was time to seal the deal and move on. I wasn't going to bother handing them over to the cops, considering that pretty much a waste of time.

"Go back to Jimmy's," I said, "and when your just guy walks in, tell him whatever you want to tell him, but make sure I don't see you around again, or you'll really get a beating."

"Okay if we tell him we did a number on you, and he figures later it didn't hold? That way we don't have to give the money back?"

"Fine by me," I said. "Whatever you want. But take your buddy there and get the hell out of my sight."

A minute later, the two of them had scampered away, leaving me with one hell of a question.

It was possible, of course, that Sean O'Flaherty had decided to work through several layers. But though I could see the mobster insulating himself from the dirty work, which made sense, I couldn't believe anyone in his orbit would think it wise to trust those two dirtbags to anything important.

Didn't feel right.

But if O'Flaherty hadn't hired them to scare me off the Thayer case, who had? Everyone's simple little open and shut murder case was starting to get really tangled and complex.

CHAPTER TWENTY-ONE

I DECIDED TO CHECK IN WITH MY CLIENT and bring her up to speed. Plus, I had a couple of new questions for her. I called Susan Thayer to see if she was home, got an affirmative answer, then headed out that way.

Driving across town, I kept a sharp lookout but didn't see any signs of a tail. Maybe O'Flaherty was giving me a day or so to think over his proposition.

Or maybe he had hired a better class of goon to tail me.

Regardless, by the time I made it to the Thayer house, I was fairly confident I wasn't being followed. Even if I had been, so what? It wasn't exactly a state secret who I was working for.

The Thayer house sat in one of the elegant neighborhoods of old Providence. Not quite the exclusive enclave of some of our millionaire class, of whom we have more than you'd think, but still an area far, far, out of my price range. Or that of practically anyone I know.

It was possible that Lt. Santiago, who seemed to live well beyond his means, had a house something like this one, but it would be a stretch even for a shady cop.

Most of the houses in this area, even though still in the city limits, sat on at least a half-acre or more of land, and they were positioned in such a way that the masses of trees and other foliage almost led one to think you were traveling through a forest. As such, the residents around here had a fair amount of privacy, at least compared to the rest of the city.

I pulled up in the driveway of a three-story, dark gray home with leaded pane front doors. A white porch swing moved listlessly back and forth in the cold winter breeze. The house had an attached garage, with the door up. Inside, I saw a red Mercedes convertible and a dark green Range Rover.

This merely confirmed that when Susan Thayer had mentioned the other day about having some independent income, she hadn't been pulling my leg. Added with a few other comments here and there, it seemed pretty obvious that she had the bulk of the money, regardless of where it had come from, in the family. Judging by my one meeting with the good professor, I would have bet anything that that really rankled him.

And I found myself wondering just where Mrs. Thayer got her money from.

As I exited the Cherokee and headed up the porch steps, the front doors opened and the lady of the manse greeted me. I nodded in return, and she ushered me into her home.

Today, she wore an ultra-faded pair of jeans and black calf-high leather boots. Her burgundy turtleneck sweater complemented those striking blue eyes of hers.

"Have you made any progress?" she asked as she motioned me through the split-level living room and to a sleek, black leather couch. She herself took a matching chair about ten feet away.

Before answering, I took a moment to survey the living room and what I could see of the rest of the house. Kind of like the outside, the furnishings were tasteful, obviously way expensive, but not flashy or showy. Same with the cars outside. If I'd had to bet, I would have guessed that, even beyond financing, Susan had done most of the purchasing and decorating in the Thayers's lives.

"There's been some stuff happening," I told her, "but I'm not sure if you'd call it progress."

"Okay."

"When I visited your husband the other day, he didn't seem particularly thrilled that you'd hired me."

Susan Thayer lowered her eyes, and a bit of a blush appeared on her cheeks. "I know," she said. "He called me later that night. I'm sorry about that. I didn't think he'd react that negatively to someone attempting to help him."

"Any idea why he was so bent out of shape?"

She smoothed her hands down the length of her thighs.

Lucky thighs, I thought.

"I guess it's just his way. Felix has always been—headstrong—I guess you'd say. He has to always be right and in charge."

"Meaning he saw me as a threat of some sort?" I asked.

"Possibly you threatened his notion that he could get himself out of this. That he sees his current situation as a challenge only he can overcome."

"Could that also be why he hired Lancaster?" I asked. "I also had a visit with him, and I agree with you. He's way out of his league on a capital case."

"You met Mr. Lancaster?"

"I stopped by his place to get acquainted."

Susan Thayer shook her head and slumped her shoulders. She had the look of a woman whose life had completely upended on her, which was actually about what had happened.

"I'm beginning to believe I'm handling this all wrong," she said. "I tried to talk Felix into letting me pay for better legal counsel, which he refused. Then I hired you, even though I wasn't entirely sure how it would work out, and he resents that."

"What else does he resent?" I asked.

She looked up at me, confused, and I spread my arms to take in the living room. "Hard to justify all this on a professor's salary."

"I told you that there was money from my side of the family," Mrs. Thayer said.

"That you did. And I'm wondering about how much you have and how much it eats at your husband."

She frowned and drummed her fingers on the arm of her chair. "Come to think of it, it's kind of odd. Felix never seemed to resent my money before, but now it's like it's toxic to him."

"How long have you been married?" I asked.

"Excuse me?" She pulled back a couple of inches into her chair, almost as if I'd approached her with menace.

"I need to know as much as I can to make sense of all this," I said. "How long have you two been together?"

"We've been *together*, as you put it, for almost five years. Married for a little over three."

It didn't take long to do the math on that and come up with my next question. "I'm guessing not the first marriage for either of you?"

"This is getting really personal for me, Mr. Quinton."

"I understand. But look at it from my point of view. Your husband may or may not have committed the crime he's charged with. In order to for me to determine which, I need as much data as possible."

"But what could something from either mine or Felix's past have to do with—"

"I don't know until I know. How about answering the question?"

She seemed to deflate a little as she looked away from me. "Second marriage for me. The fourth for Felix."

Okay, not quite what I'd expected. "Divorced?

"I am—was—a widow. My first husband, Major Jack Tallott, was killed eight years ago in Afghanistan."

I suddenly felt like a crud.

"Felix's' previous wives," she continued, "form a mix bag of graduate students, bartenders and, I believe, one mother of a student of his."

I was starting to understand what the younger crowd these days meant by TMI.

"Do you want names, ages and reasons for divorce?" she asked.

"Not now. If it becomes relevant later on, yeah, I'm afraid I'll need to know all that."

"Whatever." The dismissiveness in her tone practically slapped me in the face.

"What were you thinking when you came to me?" I asked.

She spread her hands, palms upwards. "I guess I was expecting you to dash to the rescue and prove my husband innocent. But that was shockingly naive, wasn't it? That kind of thing only happens in the movies, right?"

"Most of the time," I said. "But in this case not necessarily so."

Her eyes lit up, and she sat up a little straighter. "What have you found? Do you believe Felix is innocent?"

"As for that, I have no idea. But it's pretty obvious that there's more to this than it seems at first."

"How so?"

"Do you know, or have you ever heard Felix mention, a man named Sean O'Flaherty?" I asked.

She wrinkled her forehead, as if searching her memory for the name. "No," she finally said, "I don't recall anyone by that name. Should I?"

Okay, then. Another piece of the puzzle had just fallen into place. I now knew two things about this case.

One, while I wasn't sure of the shape or dimensions, there was a puzzle to solve concerning the murder of Michael Hartness. I couldn't bring myself to imagine that it was as cut and dried as the cops seemed to think.

And now I had another little mystery to solve. Because no matter what skills or talents Susan Thayer possessed, I now knew one thing for certain,

She was a terrible liar, and I hate it when clients lie to me.

CHAPTER TWENTY-TWO

BEING THOROUGH, I DECIDED TO CHECK into Felix Thayer from the other end of the spectrum, even though it would make me feel a little creeperish. I wanted to talk to some of his students, get a feel for how he acted in the classroom, and maybe out of it, with them. Not being all that conversant with how colleges work, I made a mistake right off the bat.

I called Felicia Adams and explained what I wanted.

"No way, dude. That's a line I can't cross. Student records are beyond confidential. If I gave you names and info like that, I'd be in big trouble."

"From the chancellor?" I asked.

"No. From like the federal government."

Okay, that way was out, which left me falling back on Plan B, hanging around outside of Thayer's various classes and trying to interview students I saw leaving. Under ordinary circumstances, I figured that it wouldn't be that hard to go through the school's online catalog and find out when and where Thayer's classes met, but the current circumstances were far from ordinary.

"Tell me this," I asked my favorite inside informant, who hadn't yet hung up, "what's going on with Thayer's classes since he's currently—uh—indisposed?"

Felicia stayed silent for a heartbeat or two, no doubt pondering whether answering that would violate some form of confidentiality.

"Ordinarily," she said, "if someone has to they can easily cancel a class with no problem. Especially if they're an associate prof."

"Okay."

"But that's for a one-off situation. If something comes up long term, like an illness or something, they usually try to get one of the other profs to cover. And if they can't, the school calls on an adjunct."

"Adjunct?"

"A part-timer," she said. "Someone who comes in to teach only one or two classes."

"What are they doing during Thayer's—absence?"

"Right now, there's a couple of adjuncts filling in, seeing as they obviously don't know for sure yet how long he's going to be out."

"Classes being held same days and times?" I asked. "No change in schedule?"

"Yep. Be too much of an imposition on the students if they rescheduled everything."

A couple of hours later I was loafing around outside one of the university's two engineering buildings. Why a class on Social Ramifications of Gender Theory, whatever in the heck that meant, was held in an engineering building rather than in the social sciences hall, I had no idea. Didn't really matter because I was more interested in the people who would be exiting the place around seven o'clock.

Checking his schedule had revealed that Thayer was actually listed as only teaching two classes this semester. Considering that someone of his rank was probably pulling down around eighty grand a year, it seemed to me like a pretty darned cushy type of job.

I parked myself on a green metal bench across the way from the building's front door and waited. I considered it a good chance that other classes would be letting out about the same time, but detective work often involves asking the same question eighty or ninety times until you get the answer you want, and just as often the answer you don't.

And if I didn't track anyone down, I'd come back the next time Thayer's class met or try his other course this semester.

About five minutes till seven, the metal doors opened up, and a group of around twenty people, most but not all of them looking early to mid-twenties, came streaming out. Although they were separated in groups of ones and twos, there was a kind of cohesion to the group that gave me the impression they were all coming from the same place, so I stood up and walked over their way.

As I did walk over, I scanned over the entire bunch, looking for possibly the best person to approach.

I at first discounted the seven or eight lone females, as practically nothing can be more off-putting to a young woman than to have a strange man, especially one dressed like a longshoreman, approach and begin asking random questions. Maybe if I was ten or fifteen years younger, and dressed a little more upscale, I would have given it a try.

Three of the men got scratched off right away as well. Big, beefy and with spiked crewcuts, I was willing to bet that they were football players, or jocks of some kind, and they were taking a class on the sociology of gender whatever only because they'd been somehow forced to. As such, the impressions they had, if they bothered to have any, of the teacher would be seriously slanted in a particular direction, and I wanted as much unfiltered information as possible.

It took only about forty seconds for me to home in on a group of four, two guys and two girls, all looking in their early twenties, who had broken off from the rest of the pack and, instead of heading to the nearest parking lot, angled off in a direction that would take them across the street and off campus.

On the far corner in the direction they headed stood a forty-year-old building that housed a small bar called Gino's with some of the best pizza in town. Because it seemed clear the four were going there for an after-class dinner, I tagged along.

I waited about five minutes after they entered before going in myself, and it only took a second to spot the four of them sitting at a booth in the far back. They were all reading menus, and as I spotted them a young, blond waitress was setting a pitcher of beer on the table. As the waitress walked off, I sauntered up to their booth.

"Excuse me?"

All four looked up. The two girls could have been interchangeable, blonde and blue-eyed. Sitting down it was hard to tell their height, but I figured them at around five-five or six. One had pierced ears, and the other had a small ruby nose stud.

Of the two men, one I guessed at around six feet tall, with the other quite a bit shorter. The taller one had brown hair already beginning to recede, while the other had black hair cut into a thick crew cut. Something about their bearing, even sitting down in a pizza bar, almost screamed ex-military.

"Yes?" asked the taller guy.

"I wonder if I could ask a few questions," I said.

"You taking a survey or something? We're trying to eat here, man."

"Not a survey," I said. I pulled out my wallet and showed my investigator's license. All four of them craned forward to check it out.

"No kidding," the tall guy said. "An actual private detective?"

"That's the reaction I usually get."

"So where's your gun?" the kid asked.

"Out in my car."

"What do you drive? A 'Vette? A Porsche?" one of the girls asked.

"Jeep Cherokee," I said, and they all seemed to deflate a little.

"What do you want?" the shorter man asked.

"You guys just come from Prof. Thayer's class?"

All four nodded, as if they'd guessed all along that my presence had something to do with their murderous teacher.

"Yeah," the tall guy said. "You want to talk to us about him?"

"If you don't mind."

They looked at each other for a second before the tall guy, obviously the unofficial leader of the group, nodded.

"Pull up a chair then and ask your questions."

As I was sitting down, the waitress came by and took their order for two large pizzas, sausage and mushrooms on one and something called a Big Mo Mudslide for the second, plus another pitcher of beer. After the waitress left, they sat watching me expectantly.

"A Big Mo Mudslide?" I asked.

The two girls giggled. "All meat, double of everything, and not a vegetable to be found," said one of them.

"Okay."

"You going to ask us if we think he killed his wife?" the shorter man asked.

"No."

"Oh." All four looked rather disappointed at that. "Why not?"

"Because I'm assuming that someone as intelligent as Dr. Thayer wouldn't make it obvious to a bunch of people he doesn't know all that well that he had homicidal tendencies."

They all looked impressed, although whether it was because of my logic or the fact that a guy who looks like me used the phrase "homicidal tendencies" I wasn't sure.

"Is this your first class with him?" I asked.

Three of them nodded, but one of the girls shook her head. "Naw, I'm majoring in soc. I've had a couple of courses with him."

"What's he like?" I asked.

She glanced at her three friends before turning to me. "As a teacher?"

"Of course."

She shrugged and looked a bit embarrassed. "I've had worse."

"How much worse?"

She drummed her fingers on the table for a minute. "Not too much worse."

"Anything specific?"

Before she could answer, the other girl spoke up. "Professor Thayer's a douche," she said.

"How so?" I asked, wondering if that word was verging on being overused.

"How would you think a teacher could be a douche? Thinks he's God's gift to everything. He's the smartest one in the world, and if you dare disagree he cuts you down in front of everyone."

"How often would he do that?" I asked.

"All the time," the shorter guy chimed in. "Almost made a ritual of it. Every class period seemed to pick two or three people out as the ones he was going to demean that day. This late in the semester, he was already on his second round of insults."

"How was he on grading your work?"

A round of shrugs greeted that one. "How could we know? He's a big shot. You think he wasted any of his precious time with his students' work?"

I talked to the youngsters for another ten minutes or so, but mainly got more of the same. One of the girls mentioned that Thayer occasionally looked at her like a creeper, but the one who'd had several classes from him interjected that that was his usual look all the time. The overall impression I got was that the good professor wasn't all that well loved by his students, on top of his co-workers and university staff.

I thanked the kids for their time and headed out to the parking lot where I'd stored the Cherokee. As I walked, I mulled over everything I'd learned about Thayer in the last few days, none of it complimentary, but none of it also directly indicating him as a potential murderer.

There did seem to be something dangling just beyond the edge, something having to do with his relationship with Hartness, that no one wanted to talk about. It could be nothing, an example of people insulated in their own little world blowing something completely out of proportion, or it could be the missing piece of the puzzle that would either clear Thayer or seal his fate.

So far, the motive for the crime was still unknown, and while almost everyone agreed that Thayer was a kind of scummy guy, there was still nothing to indicate he was capable of, or inclined to, murder.

Least of all the kind of savage, no-holds-barred killing he was charged with.

There had to be something else, but at the moment I wasn't quite sure where to begin looking.

Pulling out of the parking lot and turning to the east, it took me no more than a couple of seconds to spot a maroon SUV parked about half a block down the street.

As I went by, the two men inside looked away, and a couple of minutes after I passed they pulled away from the curb.

Uh huh.

CHAPTER TWENTY-THREE

For a while, I drove aimlessly, hither and yon, moving across Providence in no clear pattern. The maroon vehicle would disappear for a while, but sooner or later it always came back into view. During the times it vanished, I kept my eye out for a second tail car, and while I kind of wondered about a blue Mustang that briefly appeared alongside me, I couldn't find any concrete indication of multiple vehicles.

All of which could mean anything or nothing. It could mean that O'Flaherty thought little enough of my skills that he figured one car was enough.

Or it could mean his own people weren't all that practiced when it came to surveillance.

Or that I really wasn't sharp enough to catch a second or third car.

Whichever, as I drove along, taking care not to make any sudden turns or lane switches, I felt a little cranky about being constantly followed. I pulled out my phone and placed a call, hoping that the person on the other end was able to take calls at the moment.

"Yeah, what's up?" Sgt. Josh Nichols growled.

"How's it going, buddy?" I asked, keeping my voice intentionally light.

"How it's going is I'm walking on eggshells around the lieutenant. What the hell did you say to him now?"

"Nothing, that I know of."

"You still messing around in the Thayer deal?"

"My employment status hasn't changed since yesterday."

"Uh huh. Well I hope you're calling to invite me to dinner some night, or to tell me you've found the love of your life and I've just got to meet her. Other than that, I don't have time to . . ."

"O'Flaherty," I cut my cop buddy off. "Where can I find him?"

"Before I say anything," Nichols replied, "I've got a question of my own."

"Shoot."

"Why in the hell would you want to find him?"

Braking as I pulled up to a red light, I glanced in the rearview. Yep, the tail car was hanging back there.

"Two reasons," I said. "One, somehow or other he's connected to the Thayer thing. And I'd like to know how and why."

"Uh huh. And the second reason?"

"I think I've got a couple of his boys on my tail, and I'm getting a little bit tired of them dogging me around."

"You sure it's Sean's boys? You've pissed off one or two people over the years, you know."

"Funny you should mention that," I said. "I had to accost a couple of guys outside of the station this morning."

"Accost as in beat up?"

"Accost as in defend myself. I picked up their tail as I left after talking to your boss, who by the way all I asked him to do was look into some evidence for me."

"That would do it. There's nothing he likes better than having civilians coming into his office and telling him how to do his job."

"Yeah, well, everyone needs a hobby. Any rate, after I left I found these two low-rents following behind me and we had to have a conversation."

"And?"

"And nothing. I assumed they were Sean's boys, but they denied it."

"Which you accepted at face value and let them go, right? Otherwise, if they wanted to make a deal out of it there's one or two charges we could bring against you."

"Come on, Josh. The last thing on their mind was calling the cops into it. But if you must know, I asked them kind of forcefully, and they still said they didn't work for O'Flaherty."

"But he could have hired them through a middleman," Nichols said. "If for some reason he didn't want his fingerprints on it."

"True. But it's still kind of odd. After his visit to the Blaster we already know he's interested somehow. I just want to check in with him to see if it's his boys following me."

"And if it is?"

"I was thinking of making their work easy and giving them my itinerary for the next few days."

Nichols sighed. "Sounds like as valid a plan as any. You ever been to Leo Lou's place?"

"The Double L? Not yet. Never yet had the urge to have to douse myself in disinfectant afterward."

"Yeah, well, to each their own. The latest intel has it that's where Sean's holding court most days."

"For real, Josh? What's an up and coming mobster doing hanging out in a scumhole like that?"

"Would you have thought to look for him there?"

The light turned green, and I eased into the intersection. "You got a point," I said. "But if it's such a masterstroke, how do you guys know about it?"

"Maybe because we're a crack team of supersleuths."

"Or maybe because you've got a snitch inside his gang," I said.

"Could be that also."

"Okay," I said, "I'll give it a shot."

"On your own? Where do you want me to send the funeral bill to?"

"Come on, Josh. You know what a sweet talker I can be. What's the worst that could happen?"

I switched off before Nichols could answer and put the phone back in my pocket, then made a sudden right turn that would take me to the far northern fringe of Providence. I didn't bother looking in the rearview any more, as I saw no reason to keep tabs on my tail.

After all, I figured sooner or later we'd both end up at the same place.

CHAPTER TWENTY-FOUR

THE DOUBLE L WAS ONE OF THOSE PLACES that every town, no matter the size, has at least one of. The smaller the town, the more they tend to stand out.

When I spent my time living and working in the St. Louis area, before blowing out my knee for the third time and giving up on my wrestling career, I spent my nights in quite a few holes just like the Double L. Several times before my short, ill-fated marriage, and even sometimes during said marriage.

Probably the reason it was short and ill-fated.

But in a city like St. Louis, or Chicago, Houston or New York, the Double L's of the area tend to fade into the background, accepted as a fact of life by the denizens who frequent them, and most of the time not even known to those who don't. In a town the size of Providence, year-round population right around the 100,000 mark (not counting our annual droves of university students who lemming their way in and out) such places tend to stand out.

I pulled into a rutted, pitted parking lot that had probably last been surfaced around the time of the Kennedy assassination. There were actual honest-to-God slabs of asphalt jutting their way out of the ground, and it took about three minutes of maneuvering to get the Cherokee parked without blowing a tire.

I hoped my work inside went peacefully because if I ended up having to leave in a hurry things could get dicey.

With the night just beginning to come on, there were only a few other cars parked in the lot. That didn't necessarily mean anything because the bar was within walking distance of a couple of trailer parks and a low-rent housing subdivision, and I guessed that most of the clientele lived within walking distance.

The building itself looked as if it hadn't been cleaned or painted since the last time the parking lot had been paved. Squat, one story in height, made of blackened wood and grimy bricks with tiny, narrow windows spaced across the front (grimed over, naturally), it looked about as far from an inviting place to while away a few hours in relaxation as one could imagine. However, judging by the overall neighborhood, I had the feeling that most of the customers were there to forget their lives more than to relax.

Stepping out of the car, I took a minute to grab my gun and holster from a door pocket and slip it on under my coat. Feeling a little more secure, I buttoned up the coat and headed in for a talk with the big man.

The hinges on the door squeaked as I entered, and I blinked a couple of times to moisten my eyes.

Obviously, the proprietor of the fine establishment had never heard that Carson County had a no-smoking ordinance.

The place was about half full, a bit surprising for that early in the evening, but looking at the slouched, almost entirely male bunch, I had the feeling some of them had already been at their serious drinking for hours.

There was hardly any movement in the place, except for one booth in the far back where two men stood on each side, and as I stood there watching, I noticed a fairly constant stream of men going singly, one at a time, back to the booth, sitting down for a while, then getting up and moving on.

The burly guy behind the bar looked at me, as if telepathically ordering me to either buy a drink or get lost. I smiled, waved at him, and headed off to that back booth.

The two standing men, wearing black suits and white shirts, glared at me from behind the most Irish-looking faces I'd ever seen.

"Help you?" said the one on the left.

"I hope," I replied. "I'd like a few minutes with Sean, if that's okay."

The left man glared at me at the same time I heard a grunt from the side of the booth facing away from me. Sean O' Flaherty leaned his head around the side of the booth and looked me over.

"Quinton," he said, his voice barely above a hiss. "What do you want?"

"Wanted to give you my itinerary for tomorrow," I said.

"Your what?"

I sighed. "Come on, Sean. If you're going to be a smooth-talking, big time gangster, at least get yourself a decent vocabulary."

"Here's some vocabulary for you, Quinton. How's bout I tell Sammy here to blow you away? We speaking the same language now?"

"Sure we are. But that would be a pretty dumb move."

O'Flaherty snickered, and his gunsel on the right cracked a smile for about a micro second. "Why? You think there's too many witnesses? I got news for you, buddy. None of these guys in here will see anything."

"I don't doubt it, but that's not what I meant. It would be dumb to do a number on me because how do you think I found you here?'

O'Flaherty frowned. "That's a good point for a punk like you. How did you track me down?"

"Talked to a friend of mine down at police headquarters. A detective sergeant. If I suddenly drop away, what do you think he's going to think?"

O'Flaherty frowned even harder, and I could see his two bruisers tense their shoulders. After a moment, the mob boss spoke again.

"What do you want then?"

"Just to talk for a few minutes. Try to come to a meeting of the minds. At the very least, I should be able to free up your manpower shortage."

"Huh?"

"Whoever those guys are who've been following me around all day, maybe we can come to an arrangement and they can go back to their normal workdays. You know, beating up hardware store owners, ripping off parking meters, stealing candy from preschoolers. You know, their regular sort of thing."

O'Flaherty shook his head. "It would probably be easier in the short run to have my boys here break you in half, but that could cause problems down the line. How much talk you thinking of doing?"

"Five minutes?" I suggested.

"Okay, then." He waved his hand expansively to the other side of the ratty booth. "You got your five minutes."

CHAPTER TWENTY-FIVE

"WHATEVER ANYONE MAY THINK OF YOU, Sean, I don't see you as the kind of guy who'd be involved with murdering a professor," I said once I'd scrunched into the booth opposite O'Flaherty.

"And what do you know about what I am or aren't involved in?" O'Flaherty asked.

"Let's not insult each other's intelligence, okay? Mainly, I think you're into earning money."

"Anything wrong with that?"

"Not a thing," I said. "And that's the point. Michael Hartness was a university teacher who probably never even brushed up against your type of enterprise. Hence, you'd have no reason to bump him off."

"Maybe I should have the boys there check you out for a wire before we keep talking," O'Flaherty said.

"Maybe they shouldn't try, or they might get hurt."

"You think you're that tough, Quinton? Just because you used to dance around a wrestling ring wearing tights and throwing fake punches at other fakers?"

"No," I said. "More like because I've been brushing up against people like you for a long time now, and I'm still walking upright."

"Maybe because you're not big enough to warrant much attention," O'Flaherty said.

"Could be. But we're straying away from the main point. I'm

having trouble seeing your interest in the Thayer matter and even less your interest in me."

O'Flaherty moved his half-empty beer mug back and forth a few times.

"I've got all kinds of interests in this town, pal, and I don't see how any of them's any of your business."

I sighed, as loudly and dramatically as I could, and shook my head. "Sean, a word of advice. If you're going to make it big time in the mob, you've got to stop sounding like you've been binging *The Sopranos*. The actual wise guys get turned off by that."

O'Flaherty glowered at me, and in my peripheral vision I could see his boys tense up. "You know," the mobster said, "there's a lot of things that can happen to a guy besides being killed."

"Oh yeah?"

"Yeah. Such as you could lose your license to operate. Or that flea-trap gym of yours could be closed by the state."

"I wouldn't do that," I said.

By now, O'Flaherty's glower was set in stone. "Yeah? Why not, Quinton? What could you do about it?"

"Me, nothing." I gave him my "let's be friends" smile from back in my wrestling days, one of my favorite expressions to use right before I sucker punched some poor slob. "But if you do that, my manager Lisa's going to come after you. And even if I'm the pushover you think I am, she eats guys like you and your goons here for breakfast."

We held our respective poses for all of a minute before O'Flaherty shook his head.

"I think you're working under a misconception, buddy. Just because you managed to buffalo Paddy O'Brien all the time doesn't mean the same works for me."

"Does this mean I'm off your Christmas card list?" I asked.

"Naw, but it does mean you're in the neutral column for now. Go on about your business, do whatever you have to concerning this Thayer matter, but don't think for one minute you can tell me or my boys what we can and can't do. If we want to follow you, that's what we'll do. If we want to leave you alone, that's what we'll do. And if we want to put you flat on the ground—"

"Yeah," I said, "I get the picture."

"And there's not a goddamned thing you can do about it. Got it?"

I wracked my mind for a good comeback, but couldn't find one. Instead, I gave him a brief nod and went my way.

Great. Now, not only was I investigating on behalf of a man that everyone hated, but I had the local branch of the Outfit breathing down my neck.

Again.

Maybe I should just hang it up and go back to running my gym full time.

Nah, I reconsidered as I hit the outside and stepped into the early evening. From everything I could see, Sean O'Flaherty and his boys would be a hell of a lot easier to deal with than Lisa.

CHAPTER TWENTY-SIX

THE NEXT MORNING I WAS AT MY DESK, signing some billing orders that Lisa had prepared, when my desk phone buzzed. It was Keri Eckland, letting me know someone was there to see me.

"A woman, Sam. A classy-looking one too. What do you think she's doing in here?"

My employees think they're pretty funny.

"Probably a bill collector," I said.

"Don't think so. She referred to herself as doctor."

I perked up at that, and told Keri to send the woman back. A minute later, Talia Sanderson walked in and looked around the room.

She was wearing wool slacks so black they were almost invisible; a light blue V-neck sweater that looked, to my inexperienced eyes, to be cashmere; and a black leather coat.

"Interesting office," she said after a moment's inspection.

"Well, it's not as classy as a faculty cubicle, but it suits me."

She laughed. "May I sit down?"

"Sure." I gestured to one of my client chairs. She took the coat off and stretched out in the chair.

"Want some coffee?"

"No thanks. Just came from a department meeting, and I'm already coffeed out for the day."

I nodded and stayed quiet, waiting for her to get to the reason for her visit.

"What's that?" she asked, pointing above and behind me. I didn't have to look around to see what she meant, figuring she'd noticed the one item that catches most people's attention the first time they come in my office.

"That's my championship belt from the Midwest Wrestling League."

She gave me a faintly surprised look. "You were a wrestler?"

"Yep, for a while."

"I've never met someone with that—occupation."

I smiled at her discomfort. "Most people haven't."

"It sounds like an interesting life," she said.

"Sure, if you're turned on by scummy locker rooms, having to visit the chiropractor once a week, and upset fans throwing beer on you."

"Sorry, but I never followed any of that. Were you a big star?"

I wondered what she was really in my office for. It surely wasn't to talk about my seedy past, but I kept on humoring her.

"In a small pond. I worked in one of the major promotions for about half a year or so, until my knee blew out for the third time."

"Did you have a fancy name?"

I grimaced. "They called me The Blond Bomber."

She peered a little closer at me.

"I had a lot less gray in the hair back then," I said.

She smiled at that, and I felt my blood pressure rise a couple of degrees.

"What color of outfit did you wear?"

"I'd rather not say. If I told you, I'd probably pass out from embarrassment."

Her smile broadened.

"You've chosen some unorthodox careers," she said.

"That's one way of looking at it, but while we're sitting here chatting, Dr. Sanderson, why don't you get to the reason for your visit?"

She gave me a grin and leaned back in her seat. "You're fairly direct, aren't you Mr. Quinton?"

"I've found it usually helps speed things along."

"No doubt. You've been working hard the last few days."

I stayed silent, though I had a hunch where she was going.

"And talking to a lot of people around the university."

"One of the nice things about it being a public facility," I said. "Anyone can come on campus and go wherever they want."

"Of course, and no one's saying differently, but—"

"But?"

"But some people are becoming a bit concerned. They're worried that you—"

"Am I giving the place a bad rep?"

She grinned. "Not that so much. Though I'll admit that Chancellor Withers is more than a little concerned. It's bad enough that one of our top professors is charged with murder, but to have a private detective hanging around trying to dig up information impresses Dr. Withers as kind of—"

"Seedy?" I supplied.

"I'm sure he'd say more like unnecessary."

"I'm sure he would. But he should remember that the operative word there is charged. To date, Thayer's nowhere near a trial, let alone a conviction."

"Trust me, Sam, we're all aware of that. I just thought I'd give you a heads up that you're not exactly the most welcome man on campus at the moment."

"Message received," I said, at the same time feeling a bit of a glow at the fact that she'd addressed me by my first name.

She paused, frowning down at the floor before looking back up at me. "That being said, what have you found out? Made any progress?"

I hesitated, weighing my options. On the one hand, the university wasn't my client. From that angle, Talia Sanderson not only had no right to any info I'd accumulated, it was a potential violation of my license to share it with her. On the other hand, she seemed to be a somewhat friendly face, at least as far as the institution was concerned, and it seemed more and more likely that the motivation for Felix Thayer's actions, if indeed he was guilty, involved said institution.

In the end, I decided to split the baby, as my mom used to say.

"Is that the reason you're handling this in person, rather than with a phone call?" I asked.

"Actually, yes. The question's coming from me, not from administration."

"I can't get into specifics with you. But I can safely say that Professor Thayer isn't exactly the most beloved person on your campus."

She nodded, then paused, her lips pursing. "I believe I intimated as much when we spoke."

"You did."

"And the only reason I didn't speak more directly was because I was sure you would hear that all over."

"I did. Most notably from your chancellor. Odd he wasn't all that concerned about confidentiality or libel actions when he and I talked."

"But if you think hard, I'm willing to bet Withers didn't give you any specifics. Just a direction to look in."

"He gave me a whole lot of directions. But I get the feeling that you came here for another reason besides just picking my brain."

She kept on doing the thing with her lips, her eyes narrowing at the same time. I waited, giving her the time to work out whatever she had to work out.

Didn't take long before she sat up a little straighter and nailed me with those eyes. "If I were you," she said, "I'd go back a little further."

"Huh?"

"Look back a year or so and see what you find. Then proceed however you see fit."

"This have anything to do with the Outfit?" I asked.

"The what?" Her eyebrows arched almost into her hairline.

"Had a couple of encounters the last few days with some of the local bully boys. The type whose bosses live out of state and don't exactly have straight noses. Makes me wonder if you don't have more problems on your campus than one possibly homicidal professor."

"Oh my God! Were you hurt?"

As far as I could tell, her shock was genuine. I'd figured her having any connection with O'Flaherty was a stretch, but I'd had to ask.

"Not yet," I said, "but they sure do seem awfully interested in our boy Felix and what happens to him."

Talia stood up and pulled on her coat. "I don't know anything about that, Sam, but if you need to find a motive for Dr. Hartness's murder, you may want to look a ways back in time."

I let her get all the way to the door before responding. "Talia."

She turned back my way.

"I'm not going to do the university's dirty work for them," I said.

She smiled, and a look that I could only read as approval came into her eyes. "I understand. But make sure you don't do anyone else's."

CHAPTER TWENTY-SEVEN

It took me about ten minutes at the computer to begin to get an inkling as to what Talia had been referring. It took at the most another half hour before I wanted to push my fist through the wall as a reaction to my incompetence.

Instead, I made a call to headquarters and caught Josh Nichols at his desk.

"A grad student at the university named Jacob Wind committed suicide last year," I said by way of opening.

"I know," Nichols said. "We were kind of wondering when you were going to catch on to that."

"Why don't I remember this? It seems like it was pretty big news at the time."

"If you look at the dates, it happened right around the time you were dealing with the Nicky LeBow thing. You may recall, you were kind of preoccupied during all that. How did you come across it?"

"Did something I should have done at the beginning," I said. "A quick Google search for Felix Thayer, and up it comes."

"Odd. He really had nothing to do with it."

"No, except he was Wind's graduate advisor. Means his name was buried way down in a couple of the initial stories."

"Okay," Nichols said.

"Everywhere I go in this thing, people are hinting around about Thayer's creepiness. Now I may know what they mean."

"A secondary connection like that isn't proof of anything," Nichols pointed out.

"Yeah. But it sure as hell may add to the creepiness factor."

"How so?"

"The way I hear it, one of Thayer's hobbies was belittling and humiliating his students every chance he got. Maybe he took it one step too far this time."

"Still a stretch," Nichols said. "Unless you have proof of something."

"Any indication at all that Thayer may have been somehow involved?" I asked.

"In the kid's suicide? Not that I recall. It was pretty cut and dried."

"Hmm," I said with emphasis.

"What's hmm mean?"

"Means I'm using my brain for a change."

"What are you thinking, Blondie? You saying that Thayer may be pulling a twofer here?"

"Not that so much. Let's just say that certain elements out at the university seem to be looking for a reason to cut the guy loose. At first, I thought it was just petty politics, but now I'm wondering if there's a dark cloud of some kind really hanging over the guy."

"If that's the case, why don't they just fire him and be done with it?"

"He's got tenure, Josh," I said. "How easy is it to fire a cop once they're past their probationary period?"

"I see what you mean."

"Talking to some of his students, it's possible Thayer's a serious head case, and if he is, he may have had something to do with the Wind kid's death, whether he pulled the trigger or not."

"Kid died by hanging," Nichols said.

"Figure of speech. Though the fact he was hanged suggests an entirely different possibility."

"It does. But there was no evidence on that call either. He was fully clothed and no trace of—you know—"

"Okay, then. But that doesn't rule out the possibility that Thayer was somehow involved."

"Still seems a stretch to suggest the two are linked," Nichols said.

"There is one way they could be connected."

"Which is?"

"You've met Thayer, Josh. Talked to him."

"Yeah?"

"Wouldn't you agree with me that he thinks he's about the smartest guy around?"

"That's putting it kind of mildly, but so what?"

"Maybe," I said, "he gets off on proving, at least to himself, just how smart he is. And what better way to do that than get away with murder."

"Could be," Nichols said, "or it could be that your client's one of those people who naturally attract darkness to their lives."

"Thanks for the cheery thought, buddy."

"Any time," Nichols said.

CHAPTER TWENTY-EIGHT

THROUGH A COMBINATION OF SHREWD DEDUCTION, meticulous attention to detail and dogged perseverance, plus planting myself outside of Bevier Hall for about half an hour, I met up with Felicia Adams as she was leaving for her lunch hour.

As soon as she spotted me, she did a half turn and headed in my direction.

"You looking for me?" she asked.

"As a matter of fact, I was. Lunch?"

Felicia cocked her head at the same time a gust of March wind caused her to cinch the collar of her wool coat tighter around her neck. "Need more information?"

"If I said yes, would that be a deal breaker?"

"Hell, no," she said, "but you'll be the one buying lunch."

"Deal," I said.

It turned out her destination, a local establishment of a national burger franchise, was within walking distance. At least, walking distance if you didn't mind freezing. As we made our way, I had to fight to keep my teeth from chattering and my shoulders from hunching. Felicia was walking along, chattering away, not even seeming to notice the cold after that initial cinching of her collar.

It took almost all my willpower to keep the cold from getting to me. Sometimes living up to a he-man image feels like more trouble than it's worth.

By the time we sat down, me with a small burger and small fries and Felicia with a triple bacon cheeseburger and large fries, it was time to get down to business.

"What's on tap today?" Felicia asked. "I think I've told you about everything I have to tell the last few days. You making any progress?"

I stared at her for a heartbeat, keeping my expression as neutral as possible, before dropping the name.

"Jacob Wind."

She finished chewing for a moment before putting her burger down. "You've been busy," she said.

"Probably not as busy as I should be."

"What do you want to know about Jacob?"

"You knew him?"

"Uh huh." Her voice had dropped about half an octave in the last minute.

"From what I hear, Felix Thayer was his advisor."

"That's true."

"Bother him when the kid ended up dead?"

"How would I know? If Dr. Thayer speaks ten words to me in a day, it's a lot."

"Bother other people in the office?"

She shook her head, a glint of tear in the corner of her right eye. "Of course. You've got to understand. When someone's a grad student, they don't just pop in and out of the classroom. The professors and the grads work together quite a bit, in all kinds of ways."

"What sort of ways?" I asked.

"Research mainly. But also article writing, service work, stuff like that. Plus, most of them are teaching a couple of lower-level classes at the same time, so they're in constant contact with the actual professors."

"And Thayer was Jacob's adviser? How does that work?"

"In theory or reality?"

"Let's go with theory first."

Felicia popped a couple of fries into her mouth before answering. "In theory, the adviser serves as a mentor, kind of shepherds the student through the process. Helps them navigate the workload, as well as the political end of things. Like that. They serve basically as a shoulder for the grad student to lean on."

"Tough process?"

She almost snorted at that. "It generally comes down to two or three years of sixty-hour weeks and poverty-stricken hell."

"Okay," I said, "so that's theory. What about reality?"

She sobered up right away. "That would depend on the specific faculty advisor."

"Let's say specifically Dr. Thayer."

She mused that one over as a few more bites of her cheeseburger disappeared. Despite her general air of brashness and to hell with you all, this was definitely a woman who didn't speak without thinking things through.

"You can probably guess about how much assistance and advice he gave to Jacob."

"Can grad students switch advisers if there are conflicts?"

"They can," she said rather slowly, "but then they come off looking as if they can't take the pressure, and that never looks good."

"So if you're stuck with a bad advisor—"

"Well, it's not like you're going to flame out or anything, but the frustration can get pretty bad."

"What happened to Jacob?" I asked.

Felicia pursed her lips for a minute as she thought. "Hard to tell. I didn't know him all that well. There could have been all sorts of other issues going on with him."

"But even if there were, if Thayer treated him like an afterthought—"

"Yeah, it could have gotten dicey."

I leaned back and thought for a minute while I took a long drink of my Coke.

"This help you at all?" Felicia asked.

"Hard to tell this early on. Mainly, though, I'm beginning to wonder if Dr. Thayer has any good qualities. I mean, Christ, he's almost coming off like a character in a cheap soap opera."

"Just because he's an overall creep doesn't make him a killer," Felicia said.

"I know. But two dead people professionally close to him kind of tilts the game a little, wouldn't you say?"

Felicia shrugged and finished off her food. "Got to get back. See you around?"

I nodded as she bundled up and headed out the door. I continued sitting there, thinking about my next move, until I noticed the people behind the counter glaring at me for taking up the table.

I got up, mouthed to them "Sorry," and headed out.

CHAPTER TWENTY-NINE

IT WAS TIME TO FOLLOW UP ON A LEAD someone had mentioned earlier, so late that afternoon I was back on campus, parked outside of Bevier Hall. At that lull time between day and night classes, plus the fact of spring break right around the corner, I managed to snag a space only about fifty feet from the building.

I'd called a buddy of mine who worked in university maintenance, and he informed me that the custodial shift changes took place right around four thirty. I could have asked Felicia at lunch, but to be honest it had slipped my mind, and to be honest, if I kept running to her to clue me in to everything, she'd probably begin to think I wasn't the most professional of investigators.

Then again, sometimes, I wonder myself.

The time of day gave Bevier a kind of spooky feeling as I entered. The ground floor was entirely empty, and while from the stairwell I could hear a couple of people talking on the second floor, it kind of felt as if I had the run of the place.

I assumed there was a basement, but a quick look around the lobby didn't reveal any obvious method of getting there. I decided to take the slightly more arduous route of walking all six floors in the hopes I would run into the person I wanted and decided to start with the top three floors, the various offices, on the assumption that they would more likely be empty this early on and hence the more immediate objective of the janitors.

The fourth floor was totally empty, but about two thirds of the way down the fifth floor, I spotted a janitor's cart sitting outside of an office.

Approaching closer, I glanced inside.

There was a man in the office, running a duster over some walnut bookshelves. He looked to be in his early thirties, maybe late twenties. He wore a green uniform: dark green trousers and lighter green long-sleeved workshirt.

"Excuse me," I said.

The man turned, allowing me to get a good look at him. He stood about five eight, kind of on the slim side, but his rolled-up sleeves revealed muscular, corded forearms. He had dark black hair, barely beginning to thin, and a pretty darned impressive tan considering it was still winter.

He also had a name patch on the left side of his workshirt that read "George."

Sometimes, you just get lucky.

"Can I help you?"

"I hope so," I said. "Are you George Abbott?"

His face tightened up, just a bit, and his eyebrows narrowed together. "Who's asking?"

I'd thought of several ways to handle this, including two or three deceptions I could have possibly used. In the end, I'd decided to go with the direct approach.

"My name's Sam Quinton," I said.

"Let me guess. You're that private cop, right?"

So much for subtly flying under the radar. "You know who I am?"

"Word gets around," Abbott said as he went on with his cleaning. "You've been in and out of this place a lot the last few days. People talk."

"What do they say?"

George Abbott shook his head, then placed his duster off to the side and went out to the cart in the hallway, coming back in a minute with a rag, squeegee and bottle of cleanser.

"They say that old man Thayer killed Dr. Hartness, and nothing you say or do will change that."

"Maybe I don't want to change it."

Abbott shrugged and began working on the office windows.

After watching him a minute, I tried again. "What's your opinion of Thayer? You think he could have done it?"

Abbott turned away from his work. "Look mister, I just work here. Okay? As many people as you've been talking to, you probably know that Thayer's not that easy to get along with."

"That seems to be the general opinion.

"Yeah, well, go ahead and count me in that group."

"Meaning you don't like him?" I asked.

"Meaning just because he's got a better job than me and a couple of letters after his name don't make him a better person. Or a better man, far as that goes."

"Was it more or less on your end?" I asked.

"Huh?"

"I heard a little nugget that you and Thayer had a particular dislike for each other."

His face contorted, as if he was trying but couldn't quite get what I was saying. "I don't know what you mean by that. He didn't treat me any shittier than he did anyone else around here if that's what you mean."

"True," I said, "then again, how many other employees have keys to everyone's offices, including Thayer's and Hartness's."

That one hit home. The contorted face smoothed out and, despite the difference in our sizes, Abbott took a step into me.

"If you're saying I had something to do with what happened to Hartness, who by the way treated everyone good, say it a little louder. I'll see if I can find a good libel lawyer."

I held my hands up and took a step back. "Fair enough," I said. "I had to ask."

"And you've asked. Now how about you let me get back to work?"

It was enough for now. I could have turned him upside down a time or two, but what would that have proven? I figured he would keep for later and turned to leave.

I was halfway down the hall when Abbott called out to me.

"Hey, cop!"

I swiveled around and looked back at him.

"You're missing the picture, dude. Like I said, Hartness was nice to everyone, and I do mean everyone."

Then he grasped the cart and trundled off around the corner.

Now what the hell did he mean by that?

CHAPTER THIRTY

THE NEXT MORNING, I RECEIVED TWO PHONE CALLS before I even had my first cup of coffee. The first was from Lt. Santiago.

"We had one of our people go over Hartness's office computer," he said.

"And?"

"And did you have anything in particular you were wondering about?"

"Well," I said, "I'd kind of hoped his killer would have taken the time to sit down and dash out a quick confession."

"Then why wouldn't we have found it up and on the screen?"

"Maybe at the last minute he figured it wouldn't be too hot to confess to a brutal murder?"

"You sure you're a professional at this stuff?" Santiago asked me.

"Says so on my license. Anything special in the machine?"

"Not unless you count a whole lot of academic papers, e-mails to other academics, and details about academic conferences special."

"I'm guessing you found it all rather boring and academic."

"It took me over two hours to read through, and that was just the summary of what all our guy found. Trust me, if there was anything exciting or scintillating in there, it would have jumped out and slapped our hands."

"Scintillating?" I asked. "And you from Chicago?"

"Back there, no one ever made fun of my vocabulary," Santiago said, "cause I usually dropped them if they did."

"Fair enough. You're saying the computer's a dead end."

"At least in terms of at his office. But it was such a good idea, even if it did come from you, that we're going to go through any devices he has at home and see if anything turns up."

I thought about asking the lieutenant to keep me up to date on if they found anything, but decided against it. The man didn't care for me all that much as it was, and I figured that if I resisted the temptation to be pushy that it would keep my powder dry for later on.

After we hung up, I set to work finishing off my breakfast but didn't get too far before my phone rang again. Marveling at my sudden popularity, I picked up.

"Mr. Quinton? This is Susan Thayer."

"Good morning, Mrs. Thayer."

"I was wondering if you'd made any progress on the—the case?"

I pondered that one for a second, not sure if "progress" would be the right word to use. But she was the one paying my freight at the moment, and I didn't hesitate too long in case she might think me a tad slow in the head.

"I've gathered some information, not enough yet to make any definite conclusions."

"But is a picture forming at all?" she asked.

"It is. Although it's still kind of out of focus. Why don't we get together this morning and I can fill you in?"

She suggested a small diner that sits just off Main Street, which is actually one of the best places in Providence to grab some breakfast. It seemed a little downhill from her standard of living, though, and I wondered if maybe Mrs. Thayer was a little gun shy about being seen in public since her husband's arrest.

We settled on nine o'clock, which gave me time to run by the gym, check how the morning was going, sign a few papers for Lisa, and make it to our rendezvous on time.

Turned out I wasn't as speedy as I thought, because Mrs. Thayer was already sitting in one of the side booths waiting for me.

The Main, not the most original of names, is one of those throwbacks to Providence's earlier days as a pure college town.

Once upon a time, the various schools were practically our only industry, and everything in town catered to the student population. Things have changed somewhat over the years, in some ways for the better and in some for the worse, but there are still plenty of little pockets of the original culture if you know where to look for them.

The Main's owner Gus, a feisty old guy somewhere in his eighties by now, is best known for whipping up signature dishes, almost all of them some variation of the standard omelette, and naming them for his regulars. There are items on the menu named for various local sports stars of years gone by, several artists and writers that came out of our university, and even one for a fairly disliked local politician.

I tried once to convince Gus to do up some sort of super breakfast dish and name it The Blond Bomber, but he only gave me a weird look and asked why someone would want to eat something named after sexy movie stars.

"Bomber, Gus," I corrected him, "not Bombshell."

"What's a blond bomber?" he asked with such a straight face that I couldn't tell if he was kidding or not.

Susan Thayer was wearing a navy-blue wool coat that hit mid-thigh, a maroon cable knit sweater and gray slacks. She wore a gold watch, so expensive I couldn't tell the brand at a quick glance, on her left wrist and looked as if she were on her way to an important business meeting, a legal consultation maybe, or a real estate closing.

If you didn't know that the lady's world had fallen in on her a week ago, you'd never have guessed she had a care in life.

I slid into the booth opposite her and shook my head when the woman behind the counter raised up a half-full coffee pot. I shook my head again when she held up a menu. She frowned at me and turned away.

Mrs. Thayer held a cup of coffee in both hands, and from the lack of steam coming off it I gathered she'd been sitting there for a while.

"What have you found out?" she said in greeting.

I leaned back and gave her a look. "Among other things, I've learned that your husband isn't particularly well liked around the university."

"You're surely aware there's a lot of politics out there," she replied.

"Of course. But I'm not talking about just his colleagues or the administration. I'm talking even down to the custodial staff."

"Felix is a highly intelligent man. Such people are often—"

"Mrs. Thayer," I interrupted, "from everything I've gathered so far, Felix is an irritating, elitist snob who gets his jollies from browbeating those under him. I would call him a bully, but I happen to think that word's way overused these days."

She actually gave me a smile at that, though not a large one. "It seems to me that being unlikable isn't exactly a prerequisite to murder."

"And I'd probably agree with you, if I knew what prerequisite meant, but it also makes it a heck of a lot more likely that people will automatically think the worst of him. He doesn't have a lot of friends on campus."

"I've always assumed that."

"I also know that, for some reason, the local mob is interested in your husband."

She jerked at that one, and I saw some sort of revelation in her eyes before she managed to mask it. "Come again?"

"Mrs. Thayer," I said, "we're sitting about a foot away from each other, which means I'm pretty sure you heard me the first time. You remember the other day, when I asked you about a man named Sean O'Flaherty?"

Her lips tightening, she gave me a quick nod.

Despite her obvious personality and physical attractiveness, Susan Thayer would never make it as an actress. Even so, I decided to play along a bit.

"He's the closest thing we have these days to a local godfather. On his own, he's not much more than a two-bit hoodlum, but he's the local face for the Chicago boys."

"I'm sorry," she only barely managed to keep her voice from a quaver, "but I don't understand any of this."

Same as the day before, I didn't believe her for a minute. "Regardless, for some reason O'Flaherty's interested in your husband's case. To the extent that he's had some of his toughs following me around."

"Any idea why?"

"Nope. He came by my office the other day to trash things out, but it didn't go well."

Those lips tightened even more, and a whole new level of worry appeared in her eyes. "I have no idea why someone like that would be interested in Felix," she repeated. "Have you asked him about it?"

"Not yet, but I plan to first chance I get. At the moment, I'm asking you."

"And I've told you," she said through compressed lips, "that I've never heard of the man."

"If you say so," I said, deciding to fight that battle down the line, "but just to be clear, people in my profession are kind of like doctors. The more upfront the client is, the easier things get down the line. The more information held back, the harder it is for me to do the job you hired me for."

"I understand," she said, "but I'm not hiding anything."

Even as she said the words, her fingers began tapping her coffee cup.

"Regardless, I'm sure you know that right now things don't look good for your husband. Everything practically screams his guilt."

"I suppose the fight over the chair doesn't help his case any," she said.

I glanced at her. "The what?"

Her eyes widened. "You didn't hear about that? Who all did you talk to?"

"The top guy, several of his colleagues and an assortment of students and staff. What were you talking about?"

"They all must have decided to overlook something."

CHAPTER THIRTY-ONE

ONE, IT WAS FRIDAY MORNING.

Two, spring break officially started in about six hours.

Three, I figured the odds of actually finding anyone on campus were rather steep.

Turned out I was right. As I tooled the Cherokee down the street, I saw fewer students and more open parking spaces than I had all week.

I guessed, more from common sense than any deep understanding of how colleges work, that the majority of workers on site would come from the lower-end staff positions and anyone of any importance would be long gone.

Those who really had clout would all probably be meeting up to go skiing in Vail or someplace like that.

Thus, I was beyond surprised when I found Talia Sanderson working in her office. When I came in, she looked up and gave me a flash of the eyes.

"Hello, I didn't expect to see you for a while."

I sat down in one of the chairs without her offering, but she didn't seem to mind. "One of the worst traits of my job," I said. "Tending to show up when people either aren't expecting or don't want to see me."

"Oh, I doubt that I'd consign it to the latter," she said with something almost close to a giggle.

"Another of the bad traits is stumbling around and bumping

into things. I bumped into something today, and I thought you may be able to help me out with it."

"Then this isn't a social call?" she asked.

"Sorry, no. Maybe next time."

A full-throated laugh this time, and she relaxed back into her black leather desk chair. "What specifically are you interested in, Mr. Quinton?"

"I understand that Dr. Thayer was in the running for chair of his department."

She pursed her lips for a thoughtful moment before answering. "That's true. I'm not exactly breaking any trade secrets by admitting that. We were actually going to hold the selection vote in a couple of weeks before all of this happened."

"Tell me," I said. "Would I be going out on too far of a limb to assume that another person in contention, as you scholarly types say, was Michael Hartness?"

Those green eyes hooded, but only for a moment. "You're not quite as thuggish as you appear, Mr. Quinton. In fact, Drs. Hartness and Thayer were the only two candidates."

"Could this conceivably fall under the heading of what the cops could consider a motive?" I asked.

"For murder? A department chair? Only if one were seriously unhinged."

"It sounds like a prestigious thing," I said.

"Only to those who don't know squat about campus politics. As chair, you get relieved from one teaching duty."

"Which means they only have to teach one class every other year instead of two?" I asked.

Sanderson frowned, but I got the feeling not at me. "Your flippancy wouldn't be all that humorous if it weren't pretty much on the mark. We're a research institution primarily, and while our faculty are expected to teach classes, it's not exactly at the top of their priority lists."

"Any extra money come with being chair?" I asked.

"Most assuredly not. The main reward is about three times the headaches to deal with each day."

"Headaches concerning students?"

She laughed again, and in someone less sexy and dignified it would come out almost as a bark. "If only. Those are relatively easy to deal with. No, the headaches come from trying to corral all the egos of those who already have initials after their names."

"Let me get this straight," I said. "As department chair, either Hartness or Thayer would have no increased salary, slightly reduced teaching time, and they'd have to deal with everybody's crap?"

"You put it a little bit crudely," she said, "but that's essentially correct."

Now it was my turn to frown. "Why in the heck would anyone want that job?"

I'd meant it as an offhanded question, not really expecting a response. But I got a response, though not exactly the kind I could interpret.

Dr. Sanderson's lips compressed, and a veiled look come over her eyes.

She took a deep breath before answering. "Probably for prestige more than anything. It would look good on a resume to say you'd served as department chair, even if only for a year."

"Well, sure but," I paused as another thought percolated into my brain. It was a new sensation, and for a moment there I almost felt like a real detective. "Wait a minute. What do you mean on a resume? Both Hartness and Thayer are tenured, right? Permanent job, set for life and all that?"

Her face tightened even more. "All I mean," she paused, as if to choose her words carefully, "is that if at any point down the line, either of them would be looking to move on, it would be a feather in their cap."

I thought faster than I probably had since beginning this case, and decided not to press it at the moment, though I did file away the fact that she seemed fairly uncomfortable at the moment.

"What about gangsters?" I asked, in an attempt to divert her away from her discomfort yet keep her talking at the same time.

"Excuse me?"

"Gangsters, doctor. You know, shoot 'em up bad guys. Any

chance that either of the men in question was involved in organized crime in some way?"

She sat up straighter, and that veiled look disappeared from her gaze. "Really, Mr. Quinton, that's ridiculous. Both of those men are, or in the case of poor Michael were, esteemed members of this college's faculty. What could they possibly have to do with organized crime?"

"That's what I'm wondering, dean. But the simple truth is that ever since I was hired on for this gig I've been shadowed by assorted members of the local mob. And the other night the top wiseguy came by to let me know he'd be keeping an eye on me. Any idea why that would be?"

She spread her hands out on her desk. "I honestly can't even begin to imagine. I can assure you I never heard word of any such thing around campus."

My main reason for throwing out the mob bit was to get a reaction of some kind. And as far as I could tell, genuine puzzlement was what I got.

Which left me at square one as far as O'Flaherty and his bunch went. I cudgeled my brain for some more questions to ask, but couldn't think of any.

"If there's nothing else," Dean Sanderson said, "I have a couple of chores I need to finish before break starts."

I stood up first, saving her the embarrassment of trying to force me out, shook her hand and thanked her for her time. As we shook, I felt a slight tingle and wondered if she felt it as well

CHAPTER THIRTY-TWO

One thing I had yet to do in this case was seriously look into the victim. For obvious reasons, all of my attention had been focused on Thayer and, to a lesser extent, his relationship with Hartness. Concerning that, Talia Sanderson's revelation that both had been in the contention for a seemingly meaningless administrative post added a whole new set of questions to the mess.

When I left her office, the campus appeared even more deserted than when I'd arrived, allowing me to easily ensure that no squad of scarred-knuckled Irish hard guys lurked around ready to pounce. I managed to get to my Cherokee in relative safety, my only physical discomfort being reddened cheeks from the wind and a few spits of sleet that had shown up, and sat in my car warming up while I plotted out my next moves.

Susan Thayer wanted to know whether her husband was guilty or not, but maybe instead of trying to determine Felix's guilt, I should reverse the equation a bit and simply go about solving Hartness's murder.

Simple, sure. So simple it was probably beyond me.

I was pretty sure Lt. Santiago would agree.

A little bit of digging and a few phone calls revealed that Hartness lived, or had lived, in a condo complex on the north side of town. In mid-day traffic, it took about fifteen minutes to get there, and as I pulled into the complex's parking lot, I saw only a handful of cars scattered around, leading me to assume that most of the residents were young professionals out and about their various professions.

Hartness's unit was on the bottom level of a building that housed six. His unit was in the middle, and as I walked around to survey all the possible angles I kept a look out for any stray neighbors, deliverymen, joggers or gunslingers who may wander by.

I then did a second circuit while wondering about whether or not I should go ahead and break into his place. On the one hand, since he'd been killed at his office the unit wasn't marked off as a crime scene, and it had probably been way too soon for whoever owned the complex to even consider installing a new tenant.

This was a possible break. If Hartness had lived in an apartment, instead of a condo, there stood a good chance that, with him not even dead a week, the place would have already been rented. Especially considering how scarce rental units were in the current market.

But with a condo, you were talking an actual turnover of property, making it more than likely that little, if any progress had been made in converting over the property.

On the other hand, breaking in, even if the owner was deceased, would still technically constitute a crime.

If I entered the premises, to use cop speak, and managed to find something that cracked the case and tracked down the real killer, it would be a heck of a story to tell the guys back at the gym.

Then again, these days, half the guys at the gym, if not more than half, were actually women, and since a fair number of them worked in law enforcement and used my place because I give cut rates to first responders, they probably wouldn't be all that impressed.

And a few of them would probably love the chance to put me in my place by hauling me off to jail just to yank my chain.

Then again, I could jump onto I-70, drive to St. Louis and stop by the gym where I used to train during my wrestling days and tell them all about how I broke a big murder case, but for all I knew that place was now an outlet store, and no one there would want an over-the-hill thug hanging around.

Finally deciding I was wasting too much time, I pulled into a parking space about one building down from Hartness's, gave the layout one more quick survey to make sure there were no witnesses around, and got out of my car, pulling on a pair of thin, black leather gloves as I did so.

Five cars were parked in various slots outside his building, but I couldn't detect activity of any sort. It took only a few seconds to go around to the back of the unit and ease over to his apartment, even moving slower than normal because I kept swiveling my gaze around.

As I stopped outside Hartness's door, it suddenly occurred to me that I didn't know if he had lived alone or not. The basic news about the murder didn't mention anything about wife or family, but they wouldn't necessarily do so, and if he had something as casual as a live-in girlfriend, that definitely wouldn't make the news. Then again, if he had any kind of immediate family in the area, Josh Nichols surely would have clued me in.

I considered taking a minute to kick myself. All of the people around his workplace that I'd interviewed, and I hadn't thought to ask them such a simple question. I tried to console myself with the notion that my original focus had been to determine whether or not Felix Thayer was guilty, not who'd actually committed the crime, but that didn't make me feel a whole lot better.

Shaking my head in an attempt to physically dispel my worries, I gave the door a good once over. Not seeing any signs of a home security system, I decided the heck with it and went about opening the door.

Three minutes later, I stood inside the dead man's living room and scoped out the surroundings. Maybe I'd been mistaken, and college professors lived wilder lives than I'd imagined. The apartment was decorated in noticeable colors: red drapes, green and black furniture, all sorts of doo dads scattered around. The couch pillows were bright red, and three expressionistic type paintings on the wall presented a flurry of colors.

The place wasn't all that big, but it looked like it would serve a single man comfortably. I made my way to the small kitchenette and looked in the refrigerator, filled mainly with an assortment of foreign beers and small, individually-wrapped gourmet meals. The management obviously hadn't yet gotten around to clearing out the place. The freezer and cabinets were practically empty, leading me to believe Hartness had done most of his dining outside of the home.

I didn't know exactly what I was looking for, and it would have been cliched to say that I'd know it when I saw it. Basically, I was interested in anything that would give someone a motive for killing the man.

I walked into the one bath the apartment held, looked through the cabinets and under the sink. I found a lot of stuff, all of it tending to the notion that Hartness, at least while alive, had had an active social life. Or maybe he was one of those guys who talked a lot, acted little and believed in being prepared just in case. I found an assortment of hair products, male perfumes and, uhm, marital aids.

Could be the dude had made time with someone else's woman and paid the ultimate price for it.

Then I remembered the absolute savagery of the attack, and dismissed that possibility. A guy who'd felt cuckolded would maybe throw a couple of punches, possibly knife or shoot someone, but more than likely not go to the extremes that Hartness's attacker had.

But maybe I was thinking in terms of the wrong gender. What if Hartness had done something to piss off a woman friend? Could that explain any of this?

From the bathroom, I made my way to the bedroom and saw even more of the wild color scheme I'd already encountered. The bedspread was a crushed velour fabric in dark crimson; more abstract artworks, these merely dabs of primary hues, spackled the walls; and the dark mahogany of his dresser and nightstand appeared nearly black.

I felt as if I'd been transported back to the 1970's.

So far, in either living room or bedroom, I hadn't spotted any laptop or other portable device and wondered if the cops had not carted some stuff away, but I kept on searching.

I found out pretty quickly that if the cops had been through the place, they hadn't done a very good job of it, which didn't sound like the Providence force at all. Then again, from the getgo they'd thought they had their killer in custody (and for all I knew they were right), which could have led to the most cursory search of the victim's place.

Yet even the greenest rookie wouldn't have missed what I found in the third drawer from the top of the nightstand.

I pulled the packet out of the drawer, sat down on the crushed velour bedspread and looked the items over. Old-fashioned, to be sure, and yet they seemed to fit the 1970's disco-era atmosphere of the dead man's place. I didn't go all the way through the packet, only far enough to know for sure what I held in my hands, and while I realized another piece of the puzzle had fallen into place, I wasn't quite sure what that piece signified.

In short, I still didn't know whether Felix Thayer was guilty of murder, but I did know one clear fact.

I had some really bad news for his missus.

CHAPTER THIRTY-THREE

I CALLED MY CLIENT AND TOLD HER I had developed some information on the case. She was at home and told me to come on by.

All things considered, I could think of several things I'd rather do than meet with Susan Thayer right then. Shoving bamboo splinters under my fingernails was high up there on the list. But I'd taken the lady's money and felt I had an obligation to her.

I got to her house shortly before six. I could have arrived a whole lot quicker, seeing as how traffic in Providence on the Friday before spring break is almost non-existent, but needed to take some time to figure out my exact approach before showing up.

She greeted me at the door clad in jeans and a white tee-shirt. When I refused the obligatory offer of refreshment, we headed into the living room, where I sat in the same chair I had before.

Mrs. Thayer perched on the couch, her legs tucked under her.

"Seen Felix lately?" I asked.

She nodded, and I saw a faint glisten in her eye. I wondered if, intuitively, she had some inkling of why I was there.

"His lawyer managed to wrangle a second bail hearing this morning. Unfortunately, it didn't go any better than the last one."

"How did he look?"

"How does Felix usually look? Scornful, full of himself, convinced he's going to beat it somehow. Is he?"

"You didn't mention that Felix and Hartness were both up for the same job," I said.

She knitted her brows together. "Job? They both have a job."

"Department chair," I said. "They both had put their hats in the ring for that."

Her brows almost came together.

"You must be mistaken, Mr. Quinton."

"Why do you say that? I got it from about as high up the chain as you can go."

"Because Felix despised people like that. The entire time we've been married, all I heard him talk about was how the chairs were lazy, slothful people who got off on making his life miserable. I can't imagine that he'd want that kind of post."

"Maybe he wanted to do it better," I said.

She gave me a look.

"No," I said. "That doesn't sound like the Felix we know and love, does it?"

"You said over the phone you have something to report?" she said, a faint hope glimmering in her eyes.

"I do," I said, taking a deep breath. She and I still had the O'Flaherty matter dangling, and at some point I was going to have to insist that she come clean with me. But right then I had something more pressing to air.

"Well?"

I leaned back in my seat. "I got into Michael's apartment."

Susan Thayer, no slouch in the brains department, looked puzzled. "Is that legal?"

I held my hand up in a flat plane and wagged it back and forth. "It's iffy. I wasn't violating his rights because he's, well, dead. And there wasn't any sort of police tape or any other notice not to enter."

"Okay."

"But," I continued, "it wasn't my property, so legally I guess you could say I pulled a B&E."

"A what?"

Sometimes, I overestimate what civilians know. I guess not everyone watches all those true crime shows that are all the rage on cable these days. "A breaking and entering. I guess if they knew about it the condo company could press charges, but since I didn't take much, why would they?"

"Okay, then what," she paused, her eyes narrowing, "you didn't take much?"

"Right."

"Which means you did find something? Some sort of evidence?"

"I did. In a very old-fashioned way."

Her breath caught, slightly. If I had to guess, I'd say that she had a hunch where I was headed. "What did you find?"

I reached into my coat pocket and pulled out a sheaf of small-sized envelopes, arrayed in various pastel colors. Undoing the ribbon that held them together, I spread the envelopes, all of them missing any address or name, on the table in front of us.

Her mouth had drawn tight, and I could see the ridges in her arms and hands.

"Trying to avoid sending anything electronically, in this day and age, was pretty smart," I said, "but not smart enough."

She made no move toward the envelopes, and by now the tension in her body was so stark I was afraid she'd shatter if she breathed too hard. For several long heartbeats she stared only at the envelopes on the table, not daring to look at me.

"Have you read them?" she asked, her voice the faintest of whispers.

"Not all," I said, "but enough to get the general idea. You can see the problem this presents, right?"

She nodded, and I was afraid her neck would snap off at the motion. "It could mean motive," she said.

Yep, motive. A strong one. The one thing that had been missing in this whole deal.

I felt like twenty different kinds of bastard, but had to keep plowing ahead. "Right. In the hands of the prosecution, this would be a clincher, if they even think they need one. How long, Mrs. Thayer?"

"How long?"

"Had you and Dr. Hartness been seeing each other."

Taking a deep, shuddering breath, the lady tore her gaze from the tabletop and looked up at me. "Almost a year."

"How did it begin?"

"What's the most cliched way it could have happened?" she countered.

I thought for a moment then, despite the seriousness of the subject, couldn't help but grin. "A faculty party?"

Her eyes drooped down to the table again. "Pretty pathetic, huh? The entire social sciences department was there, practically everyone in Felix's building. Worse, it was for some award that some foundation or other had given Felix. Naturally, he was the toast of the night and got—got—"

"Stinking drunk?" I suggested.

She nodded, still not looking up.

"Then what happened?"

The way she told the story, it really was as old as time. The drunken husband acting like a clown, completely ignoring his wife. The attractive younger man with the sympathetic shoulder off to the side who made her feel like something more than an ornament.

"Did you know who he was?"

"Of course," she said. "I'd been up to Felix's office several times and had met his colleagues at other get togethers. So Michael and I were already acquainted when things—accelerated."

"For most of the last year?"

She nodded. "More or less."

"Any hint that Felix found out?"

"Nothing I could tell by either his words or manner. Then again, he's always so arrogant that if he had found out, he may not have let on simply to spare himself the embarrassment of—of—"

"I think the really old-fashioned term is cuckold," I said.

She nodded, her eyes glistening.

"But when your lover turns up murdered, supposedly by your husband, you assumed he somehow found out."

Mrs. Thayer nodded again, the glisten more pronounced.

I actually had to credit her the way she was holding it together.

"Which is why you hired me. Like you said, not to prove your husband innocent, but to find out what really happened. The truth is, though, that you pretty much assumed and just wanted things confirmed."

"Uh huh."

"I guess I should be insulted," I said.

She glanced up, puzzlement showing through the glisten. "Insulted?"

I gestured toward the envelope on the table in front of us. "You must have figured I wouldn't find out. Did you think I was that incompetent?"

"I didn't know he'd kept those. We did our best to make sure there wasn't any other trace of our—friendship. No pictures, texts or anything like that. Plus, Michael is—was—a man, after all."

"And we're not exactly known for being a sentimental species," I said.

"No."

I drummed my fingers on the arm of my chair for a minute, wondering whether or not I believed her, though in the end it didn't matter.

"I have to turn these over to the cops."

She jerked back, the cords in her neck taut as ropes, those electric blue eyes of hers now broadcasting full-bore panic. "You can't," she nearly shrieked.

"I don't have a choice, Mrs. Thayer. My professional license empowers me to investigate crimes, including felonies. But if I come across any relevant evidence, I have to turn it over to the authorities."

"But if you do that, then they—they'll assume Felix is guilty."

"Where have you been, lady? They already pretty much assume that. Doesn't matter, though. If I found something that pointed to his innocence you'd want me to turn it over, wouldn't you?"

"But you work for me!"

"No, Mrs. Thayer. I work for myself. You're just a temporary client. Withholding evidence not only puts my livelihood in jeopardy, it will just about kill any rapport I have with the police in this town. So even if I did somehow keep my license, I couldn't do a whole hell of a lot with it."

Her eyes began swimming. "But if we just keep quiet about this—"

I pointed again to the letters in front of us. "You really think this can stay hidden? You ran around with Hartness for nearly a year and think you kept completely undetected? I'm here to tell you, there may not be anyone who knows, but there's a whole hell of a lot of people who suspect something."

"We didn't run around," she insisted. "We—"

"I know," I interrupted. "I read some of them, remember? Enough to know you, at least, thought you were seriously in love, but that doesn't change things."

"What do you mean 'me at least'?"

I was beginning to feel like about thirty different types of a bastard, but I had to shake the lady and get her to see reality. For one of the few times in my life, I lied to a client.

"You don't honestly think I found evidence of only one affair when I searched his place, do you?"

If the lady had seemed tense and stiff before, she now became absolutely stone. She glared at me, almost as if wanting to scorch me on the spot.

Which she probably did.

A long, painful moment slid by with neither of us saying anything. Then she pressed her lips together and stood up. She glanced at the envelopes in front of us, and she gave me a slight shake of the head.

"Then do whatever you think's right, Mr. Quinton. But as of this moment you're fired."

And with that, she turned and walked out of the room.

I saw myself out.

CHAPTER THIRTY-FOUR

THE THAYER AFFAIR DIDN'T RANK AS my shortest case ever, but it came pretty close. I had only one thing left to do before it would be all the way out of my hands.

Two things, it turned out, as I walked out of her house and into the brisk winter evening.

Maybe three, depending on how you counted.

The most important thing was to run by headquarters and drop off what I knew, plus the letters, with Nichols and Santiago. I considered calling Thayer's lawyer and giving him a heads up, but he'd find out about the new development soon enough.

What he did with it was his business, but from my point of view a wife fooling around was a hell of a lot more motive for murder than squabbling over a promotion at the university.

The matter of Jacob Wind crossed my mind for the moment, and I considered bringing that up as well. True, as Nichols had told me the cops were already aware of the kid's death, and after our talk the other day of his connection to Thayer, but at the moment it seemed a long shot that the kid's suicide had any link to the current situation.

More likely it was simply a matter that people with the personality of Felix Thayer tend to attract all kinds of darkness in their lives, either directly or indirectly.

Though it now seemed fairly cut and dried that Thayer was in fact Hartness's killer, something didn't sit right. I had a small feeling in the pit of my stomach that I was missing something, that more to the story remained uncovered.

But as I climbed into my Cherokee, I did a pretty good job of shrugging that feeling off. After all, getting such stuff sorted out is what the cops and DA's are for, and overall they do a pretty good job of it.

As I turned out of the residential area and into main Providence traffic, however, I caught a motion in my rearview mirror that indicated the other little bit of business I had to attend to hadn't yet forgotten about me.

This time it was a dark blue Cadillac Escalade that stuck to my tail.

At least they were moving up a bit in the class department.

I briefly debated ignoring them and continuing on to the station but figured my odds at arriving there uninterrupted at slightly less than fifty-fifty. I still wasn't exactly sure about Sean O'Flaherty's involvement in all of this. For all I knew, there was some connection between him and Susan Thayer, and if there was I counted it entirely possible that after I'd left the house she'd frantically dialed him up to give him the lowdown.

Then again, maybe old Sean was really, really interested in who became chair of the university's sociology department.

Or maybe he had the hots for Talia Sanderson and thought I was trying to move in on his territory.

Naw, probably wasn't any of those.

Regardless, I could see a strong likelihood that if they sniffed out my destination something would happen to keep me from getting there in one piece. Therefore, the time seemed appropriate to try and wrap up this particular angle of the mess for once and all.

At a stoplight, I hung a right on Arena Avenue and began heading south. I even had my signal light going, making it not all that difficult for the thuggoes behind me to keep track. About half a mile down the road, I hung another right and began heading south out of town, even though that wouldn't necessarily be obvious yet.

We were now on a stretch of road where the speed limit, though still within city limits, hit fifty. Just to make sure of my hunch, I goosed the Cherokee up to around sixty-five, the traffic light enough to allow me to do so without too much fear of causing a collision, and headed straight for a stoplight about two blocks away.

I passed a cluster of small side streets holding several businesses, including about four restaurants, and zoomed past one of the three major high schools in the Providence area. Behind me, the Escalade had given up all hope of concealment and was dogging my tail as much as it could.

Not for the first time, I wished I were like a TV private eye and drove some hot, sporty coupe. If so, I'd show those goons behind me a thing or two.

But I'm too big to fit into most coupes, and if I went with a sporty convertible I'd have the headroom I needed, as long as it was a nice enough day to have the top down, but the wind would whip my long hair back and forth all over the place, obstructing my vision.

All things considered, probably just as well I drove the vehicle I did, even though I had a hunch that the Escalade had a large enough engine to outdistance me in no time on a straightaway.

But that was okay as well, because I wasn't planning on running for much longer.

Only long enough, in fact, to get into the small rolling hills to the south of town, around a few curves and, with a snap acceleration down one last straightaway, head down one of the side stations of the numerous walking trails that lace through the Providence area.

By the time the Escalade, taken somewhat off guard by my boost of speed, had caught up I had the Cherokee sideways next to the trail entrance, fortunately deserted at this time of day, and had secreted myself among the trees and shrubbery that lined a small creek.

The Cadillac stopped, the engine still running, and two men, dressed in slacks and sport shirts, got out.. Suddenly, my usual attire of jeans, tee shirt and leather overcoat, not to mention the Sketchers on my feet, gave me an edge.

Upon exiting the Cherokee, I'd snagged my gun and now held it in my right hand, down by my thigh.

Both men were medium height, one blond and the other with bright red hair. The blond dude had hair almost the same shade as mine used to be before the gray started easing in. They looked like they were in shape, but it was more health-club shape than rough-stuff shape. I figured them both at around 175, and while their faces were unfamiliar they were the same type as had arrayed themselves around Sean O'Flaherty the time he came to my office.

Both wore slacks, designer shoes and mid-length J Crew jackets. Definitely up a level in class from earlier in the week.

"Come on out of there, Quinton," yelled the blond man. "We just need to talk for a minute."

Although I was in the cover of the trail, I'm not all that much of a woodsman. Plus, with it still early evening, I had some shade or shadow to hide in but not as much as I would have preferred. And if I tried to work my way either farther back or to the side, I'd surely make enough noise to allow them to track me.

Actually, all they had to do was cross over onto the trail, make their way a few yards down, and they'd find me. Instead, they stood out there by the trailhead, the red haired one nervously slapping his leg.

Probably didn't want to get trail dust all over their Gucci's.

"Come on, man," the blond shouted out again. "You can't stay in there forever. What the hell kind of a stupid game you playing?"

A game, sure, but hopefully not a stupid one. I skittered a couple of feet down the creek bank and edged along it. A very small portion of the creek, complete with covering trees, jutted its way out and up to the trailhead, and if I could play it exactly right I'd come out alongside the two of them.

Provided they didn't move.

Or I didn't snap a twig.

Of course, the little stunt would have been easier if I hadn't blown one of my knees out three times during my wrestling career. Even so, I managed to grit my teeth hard enough to keep from squealing out in pain.

The two well-dressed goons were still hovering around the trail's entrance, no doubt deciding whether to plunge on in after me or call for a backup troop of Girl Scouts, when I reared up to their side my weapon leveled and ready.

It took only a second for them to notice me in their peripheral vision.

"Oh, shit," the blond said.

"That's about the size of it," I said. "Pull 'em out and drop 'em boys."

"Drop what?" asked the redhead.

"One more stupid question and I may start playing around to see if the sights still work on this thing. I dropped it on the floor a couple of years ago, and had to hammer the front sight back into place. Wanna see how good of a job I did?"

Shoulders slumping, both men reached behind their backs, pulled out automatics and dropped them on the ground.

"Coats off," I said.

The redhead tensed up, but in the next instant they both shucked their outerwear.

"Now back up to your vehicle," I said. "I'm guessing you know the position.

The blond's face scrunched up, as if he were about to protest. Then he took a long look at me and, taking the lead, moved over to the Escalade. He and his partner took opposite sides of the vehicle and spread themselves out in the standard pose.

Only then did I come a couple of steps closer. "I'm going to assume you're being smart and don't have any other weapons on you."

"Want us to take off our pants, too?" the redhead sneered.

I took a step closer and smacked him between the shoulder blades with my gun. It wasn't a hard smack, more of a tap than anything, but it caused his legs to buckle for a second before he got control of himself.

"What do you want, Quinton?" the blond, who seemed to be more or less in charge, asked.

"More like what do you guys want? I thought Sean and I had things ironed out the other day."

"Maybe you did, maybe you didn't."

"Nice comeback."

"Or maybe," the blond said, "you did have things evened out until you got stupid."

That had kind of been my inclination. That O'Flaherty and I had an understanding, at least as far as it went, but then I did something that got him on my case again. The question was what?

"I've been following where my case leads, just like I told him I'd do," I said. "What's he got to complain about?"

"Why not pay him a visit and ask?" the blond man shot back.

His partner was looking a little edgy, as if he were about to try something stupid. I took a step back, raised my weapon and trained it on the same spot on his back where I'd hit him.

"Just so all three of us are clear," I said, "if Red there makes a dumb move, I'm blowing him away. Got it?"

"What are you planning on doing, Quinton? Holding us here till the sun goes down?"

"Not that long," I said, as I swiveled the aim of my gun and shot twice, back to back, blowing out the two driver's side tires of the Escalade.

The blond grimaced at that. Seeing as I was sure he was used to the sound of gunfire, I assumed he was the owner of the Caddie.

"Big whip," Red sneered. "You think that's going to stop us at all?"

"No," I said, "but my next move will. Cell phones. On the ground, now."

They tensed at that. I sighed, walked around to where I faced the front of their vehicle, and flattened another tire before walking back to my original position. "Now," I repeated.

The two reached into the clothing, pulled out their phones and dropped them on the ground, right next to their feet.

"Kick them back," I said. When they hesitated, I insisted. "I'm getting kind of bored shooting tires. I may try for an arm or leg next. You know, just for variety."

Shoulders slumped, they kicked their phones back. I lifted up my right foot and stomped both of them flat into the ground.

"Tell Sean that I'm unclear what he's mad about," I said. "Far as I can see, there's nothing in this thing at all that relates to him in any way, and even if there were I'm not foolish enough to openly implicate him in anything that's not directly my business. Like I told him the other night, if he stays off my back I'll stay off his. Kapisch?"

"We'll pass the message on," blond said, "but I'm not sure how he'll take it."

"I don't really give a good goddamn how he takes it, as long as he stays away from me. But just to help cover my tracks a little more, why don't you two crawl under the car."

"Say what?"

"You heard me," I said. "Crawl under the car. That way, I know I've got some breathing room as I take off."

"We're not crawling under the goddamned car, Quinton," Red snarled. "And you're really not going to be stupid enough to shoot us here. The main road's not too far away, there's houses all around, and any minute now someone's going to—"

"You've got a point," I said. "Maybe I'll just pistol whip the hell out of you while your buddy here watches. After all, it's not like I have to worry about the two of you running to tell the cops on me, is it?"

The two glared at me for a moment, then looked sideways at each other. "No, we wouldn't run off to the cops," the blond one said, "but right about now Sean sees you as an irritation. You really think you've got the 'nads for him to take it up a step from there."

"I'll worry about Sean when it's time to worry about Sean," I said, hoping like hell that I was projecting more bravado than I felt. "Right now, you two clucks are the only ones on my radar. So what's it going to be? Messing up your clothes by crawling under the car, or going home with lumps and bruises all over your faces?

"Don't even worry about, Sean," Red hissed out, his face now almost matching the color of his hair. "You'd better be watching your back for me to jump you some day."

"You already jumped me," I pointed out. "Just now. Didn't do you a whole lot of good, did it?"

"What the hell, Mike," the blond spoke up, and for the first time I heard one of their names. "This town's not all that big. There'll be plenty of chances to do him in down the line."

They sent one more venomous glare my way. Have to keep up the tough-guy image as long as possible, after all. Then they knelt down on their knees and crawled until their heads and shoulders were under the Escalade.

"All the way," I said, "scrunch all the way in there."

I heard a brief muttered oath, probably from Red, before they elbowed themselves all the way under the chassis.

A minute later, I was headed back to the main road and back into town.

CHAPTER THIRTY-FIVE

"YOU REALIZE YOU PRETTY MUCH JUST SUNK YOUR CLIENT, don't you?" Lt. Santiago asked.

"And in less than a week on the job," Josh Nichols chimed in.

The three of us were sitting in the lieutenant's office. A few minutes ago, I'd handed the bundle of letters to Santiago, and he'd taken the time to glance through a couple of them before pushing them aside. Now he was staring at me as if he wanted to scrape me off his shoe.

I figured it was just because he didn't like working late on a Friday.

"Technically," I said for what felt like the umpteenth time, "Dr. Thayer wasn't my client. His wife was."

"Was?"

"See, Lieutenant. That's why you got to be a detective. You're quick to pick up on things."

"I got to be a detective because I didn't take crap from private licenses who don't know how to stay within the lines. Get me?"

"I got you," I replied. "And you're right. When I told Mrs. Thayer, I was going to turn these over to you, she fired me."

"Letters," Santiago said. "Who the heck would have thought in the twenty-first century a pair of lovers would be brought down by handwritten letters?"

"Actually," Nichols said, "if you think about it, it's pretty smart. Anymore, if someone suspects the other person of cheating, the first thing they check is their phones and computers. If you keep everything handwritten and on paper, it's that much more likely to be overlooked these days."

"That true, Quinton?" Santiago asked me.

"Why ask me? I don't do divorce cases."

"I was thinking more along the lines of how did these come to be in your possession," Santiago said with a glare.

"That's not really important here, Lieutenant."

"Seems to me I decide what is and isn't important."

"Maybe, but at the moment here's how it plays out. These items have been handed to you. All you have to worry about is their authenticity."

"Uh uh. I also have to worry about whether they'll be admissible in court."

"Actually, you don't." Before heading over to the cop shop I'd made a quick call to Bernie Lyman, my personal attorney and one of the sharpest criminal lawyers in the state. "If you received them from a third party, and said third party was in no way acting as an agent or representative of the police, they're fair game in court."

"You don't mind if we check that out with the prosecutors, do you?"

"No problem. Far as I'm concerned, as of now I'm done with the case."

"You've given us motive here," Nichols said, "which pretty much sews the whole thing up."

"That's what I thought, though there are a few loose ends dangling out there."

"Such as?" Santiago asked.

"Such as Sean O'Flaherty's connection to all this."

"Yeah," Santiago said. "Sergeant Nichols here apprised me of that. You sure it has to do with this Thayer mess, and not something else?"

"Such as what, Lieutenant?"

"Maybe it's some sort of holdover from the O'Brien deal last year."

By way of answer, I filled them in on my latest encounter with the boys just an hour or so back. When I was done, Santiago frowned.

"Sounds like assault and battery to me. Which I'm sure you reported right away."

"Actually, there wasn't a whole lot of assaulting going on from their end," I said. "And I'm already starting to forget exactly what those guys looked like."

Santiago frowned even harder.

"When we turn these letters over to the prosecutors," he said, "they're probably going to want to kiss you."

"They'd have to get in line."

"But when we tell them the O'Flaherty business, they'll probably want me to drop you off the top of City Hall."

"To know me is to love me," I said.

"Why don't you go play around your health club for a while, and try to keep away from any Irishmen you know. If we need you, we'll call you."

"Sounds like a plan," I said.

CHAPTER THIRTY-SIX

HOWEVER, IT TURNED OUT I WASN'T quite as done with the Thayer case as I thought. Monday morning, Lisa Nolan and I were huddled over my desk, working on the accounts receivable for the last month or so, when Daniel Lancaster walked in. With his hair every which way and his eyes reddened, the young attorney looked even more flustered than the last time I'd seen him.

"Mr. Quinton, I wonder if I could have a word with you." The slight twang in his speech I'd noticed before was much more obvious now.

"About what, Mr. Lancaster? My associate and I are kind of busy here."

"It's about our mutual client, and I really need to talk to you."

Shaking my head, I asked Lisa to leave us alone. She nodded, scooped her laptop off the desk and walked out.

Lancaster sat down, his briefcase firmly clenched in his hands.

"Your manners are slipping, counselor. And for what it's worth, we don't have a mutual client. Never did. My client was Mrs. Thayer, and she fired me last Friday."

Lancaster took one hand off his briefcase to wipe across his face. "I didn't know. I've been busy all weekend, and haven't spoken to Mrs. Thayer since the bail hearing on Friday. Why exactly did she let you go?"

I thought about it for a minute, then decided there wasn't any reason not to tell him. Client confidentiality was a consideration, of course, but when you factored in the fact that the prosecution would have to let Lancaster know about the letters ahead of trial, I wouldn't be revealing anything he wouldn't come across eventually.

I laid it out for him, pretty much how it happened except for the O'Flaherty angle. When I was finished, I expected the kid to fold up his tent and go home.

But I got a reaction I didn't expect.

"That doesn't make any sense," he said.

I sighed and shook my head. "It's called a motive, counselor. If you assume that Thayer found out about—"

"I know what a motive is, Mr. Quinton. I may be a little out of my ballpark here, but please don't speak to me like I'm an idiot."

I leaned back in my chair. "You're right. I shouldn't have talked down like that. Sorry."

"Thank you. But what I mean is that Dr. Thayer was framed for this crime."

Now it was my turn to do a doubletake. "Come again?"

"Framed. We finally put it together yesterday. That's why I've been too busy to speak to Mrs. Thayer."

"How do you mean, put it together?" I asked.

"Actually, I'm talking a bit ahead of myself." He paused and took a deep breath while rubbing his hand across his face.

"Okay," he continued, "it's like this. Felix has come up with a possible idea of who may have set him up for the Hartness murder."

"You're assuming he was set up. From where I sit, the whole thing is pretty much tied up in a bow for the prosecutor."

Lancaster grimaced, no doubt thinking how he was sitting across from the person who'd put the final knot in that bow. "According to Felix, he's been having trouble with one of his co-workers recently. Enough trouble that he's managed to convince himself that this person killed Hartness and framed him for it."

"Co-worker he's been having trouble with doesn't exactly narrow it down," I said. "That would be almost half the university directory. Who'd he mention?"

Lancaster took another deep breath. "Before I proceed any

further, I need to clarify something. You told me that Mrs. Thayer had discharged you from your services?"

"If that's law-school jargon for she fired me, that's correct?"

"Because of the letters you found, I presume?"

"You presume right, counselor. Actually, it was probably more for me turning them over to the cops, but it comes out to the same thing."

"I guess I can see her reasoning."

Despite my best inclinations, by this point I was kind of intrigued. "You honestly think someone may have framed your client? Does he impress you as the most truthful of people?"

Lancaster grinned, and for the first time in our acquaintance I wasn't annoyed by him. "Despite my age, Mr. Quinton, I'm not exactly a bright-eyed crusader. I'm well aware of the probability that this is some ploy of Felix's, but as his attorney, I'm obliged to check it out."

"Understood," I said, "but why come to me?"

"You and Felix didn't exactly get along when you met before, right?"

I grinned. I was beginning to like the young lawyer more and more. "If by didn't get along you mean he looked down on me and didn't want me anywhere near his case, yeah, that's about how it went."

"Felix has always maintained his innocence. And if he is innocent, that obviously means someone framed him by putting the bloody clothing and murder weapon in his office. As his attorney, it's a possibility I have to at least look into."

"Because the more likely reason, that he's just a world class tool, couldn't possibly be correct," I said.

"Uhm, yes." Lancaster colored a bit before continuing. "So what he's been focused on is who could have hated him enough to do such a thing."

"That's a pretty hefty list," I pointed out.

"Point taken. But it's not just who would have wanted to do it, but who would have had the capability."

Now it was my turn to breathe deep as I started to understand where Lancaster was headed. "You mean someone with access to his office?" I asked.

The young lawyer nodded.

"Who would have some idea of his schedule. When he would and wouldn't be in."

Lancaster nodded again.

"He have anyone in particular in mind?" I asked.

"He's talking about one of the night custodians. A man named George Abbott."

Truth be told, I considered the notion of Thayer's innocence a long shot at best, but long shots do sometimes come in, and when I'd talked to him George Abbott hadn't quite come off as the head of the Felix Thayer fan club.

It was a notion, to be sure. And as long as the notion was in my head, I didn't feel comfortable in turning away.

"How about I work for you?" I asked.

Lancaster flinched back, as if I'd made a move to slap him. "I don't think I can do that."

"Why not?"

"To be honest, I can't—I can't really afford you. And if I paid you out of Felix's fees, I can just imagine his reaction."

"What if I give you a special on my rates?"

"Which would be?"

"How about free?"

Lancaster frowned. "I don't follow you, Quinton. What—"

"Look," I said, wondering if this could in some way explain Sean O'Flaherty's involvement, "if I had to guess, I really doubt that Felix was set up. But on the off chance that he was, I don't fancy the idea of playing even a peripheral role in that. I'm willing to invest a couple of days in digging around some more, and I can't give you more of a cut rate than free."

"That makes sense. In that case, welcome back aboard."

"Probably should keep my involvement quiet around Mrs. Thayer. She may not see it quite the same way as you and I."

The lawyer nodded, and I noticed his grip on his briefcase handle had eased.

CHAPTER THIRTY-SEVEN

"FROM WHAT I UNDERSTAND, YOU WERE out of this," Felix Thayer said.

It was a couple of hours after Lancaster had come to visit me at the gym, and the three of us were in a conference room at the jail. Thayer didn't look any the worse for wear after well over a week in lockup.

"I was," I said, "but your attorney made an interesting pitch."

"I'm not all that sure about hiring someone else on. From what my wife said, you're rather expensive."

"I prefer to think of it as cost efficient."

Thayer turned to look at Lancaster. "In case you've forgotten, counselor, this is the guy who supplied the cops with a possible motive, even if a ludicrous one. And now you want me to hire him?"

"Mr. Quinton was only following the law when he turned over those materials. Doing any less would have put him in jeopardy of losing his license."

"Whatever. We don't need him, Daniel."

"I disagree, Felix. The cards are really stacked against you now. Having an experienced investigator on our team could only help us."

"Experienced? The man's a freakin' gym rat!"

"For what it's worth," I said, "your attorney here's offered to pay my fee."

"And just how much are you planning on charging him?"

"Pro bono," I said.

"What?"

"It's a Latin term, professor. It means—"

"I know what the hell it means. What I'm wondering is why you'd be willing to do so? You got a secret inheritance no one knows about?"

I drummed my fingers on the table, seriously contemplating getting up and leaving Thayer to his fate. But a look over at Lancaster changed my mind. The young lawyer was back in Nervous Nellie mode again, and the prospect of leaving him out to dry didn't feel right.

"No," I said. "I don't have any secret money stash anywhere. What I have is a conscience, which from everything I've learned in the last week is a hell of a lot more than you have. As I was backgrounding your case, Thayer, I didn't find a whole hell of a lot of people willing to nominate you for Man of the Year."

Thayer stood up and knocked on the door, summoning the guard, before turning back to us. "Daniel, do whatever you think necessary, but you'd better not charge me a single cent for this man's services. Got it?"

"Yes, sir."

A moment later the door opened, the guards came through, and the Man of the Year left to go back to his cell.

CHAPTER THIRTY-EIGHT

B & E TIME AGAIN, THOUGH WITH a bit more risk than the last time. Breaking into and searching a dead man's home was one thing. Doing it with the inhabitant alive and kicking is something entirely different.

Fortunately, with George Abbott working nights it would be easy to work my way in around his schedule. A call to my buddy in maintenance informed me that the custodians were working through spring break, meaning there should be no lapse in his routine.

A little routine digging gave me his address in a working-class part of town, and it only took about a day and a half of surveillance to catch him pulling his dark blue Camry out of his garage and heading off to work.

I was wearing my normal clothing, not decked out in dark black for a night's skulking around. All black clothing is great if no one's around to see, but I didn't want to be driving back and forth, not to mention moving around his neighborhood, looking like a refugee from a WWII commando movie.

Plus, blue jeans, a blue turtleneck and heavy jacket fit right in with the neighborhood.

Abbott's yard had no sign that indicated a security system, which in itself didn't exactly mean anything. Sometimes people put those signs up when they have no system, merely to scare burglars, or nosy private eyes, off. Other times, people don't have the signs announcing the presence of a very real system in order to nab perpetrators in the act.

But Abbott's house, a fairly small ranch style that looked as if it had been built around forty years ago, more than likely didn't hold anything valuable enough to warrant a monthly charge for a system.

And if I was wrong? Well, that's why I had Bernie Lyman's number always at the ready.

Took me a total of ten minutes, eight of those carefully scoping out the neighborhood, to make my way into the house. Entering by the back door that let directly onto the kitchen, I stood and waited for ten minutes, long enough to ensure there wasn't any immediate law enforcement response coming.

I pulled a small flashlight out of my pocket and began combing the property.

Unlike the other day at Michael Hartness's place, I had a little more clarity in terms of what I was looking for. While I was nowhere near sold on Thayer's belief that someone in the staff at the university was behind his problems, and even less that George Abbott was in the running for top suspect, if it wasn't me, someone else would investigate, and I preferred it be someone who wasn't taking money from the man.

Plus, there was another wrinkle to consider.

If Abbott was, in fact, Hartness's murderer, he'd left all the evidence behind at the scene. It wasn't as if I was going to find a literal smoking gun, or souvenirs from the victim or even early drafts of a strongly-worded "I'm going to get you" message. If Abbott was behind the act, he would have done it pretty much as Lancaster laid out: grab the ornate paperweight from Thayer's desk, sneak into the victim's office, and do him in. Thus, there'd be no reason for any sort of evidence to be laying around his house.

But there's such things as thoroughness and professionalism, both of which dictated that I scope out the suspect's residence for any clues.

And lo and behold, I found one.

As far as I could tell, Abbott was as working class as working class can be. Yet even the bluest of blue collars own some sort of home computer, and Abbott was no different. I found his machine tucked away in a corner of his bedroom and sat down to begin working my way through it.

Fortunately, like a lot of people today, Abbott kept his machine on all the time and, even more, up and running to his page, so I didn't have to try to figure out any sort of password to get in.

Turned out that trying to figure out a password would have at least given some excitement to the whole thing. Almost an hour later I stood up, locked my hands over my head and stretched, grumbling to myself that I'd just wasted a whole lot of time.

Abbott had no hidden files, no juicy secrets buried anywhere, and absolutely nothing on his machine that implicated him in a murder/frame plot.

I was beginning to think that I'd been sold a bill of goods, that Daniel Lancaster had jumped at any chance to convince himself of his client's innocence in his first big criminal case. However, since I was already here, might as well be thorough, which meant going through the rest of the house.

I determined Abbott was a KC Royals fan, that he liked to have framed pictures of birds all around his place, and that he probably lived a rather monkish existence, as I found no evidence of any sort of feminine touch in the place.

It was simply a laborer's home, pure and simple.

At least, until I got to the garage.

It was a small, attached space off the side of the house. A metal screen door led from the kitchen into the garage, which was barely large enough to hold a gleaming, red, almost brand-new F-350. It wasn't that the garage was so small as that the truck was so big, and I stood there wondering for a moment at the concept of a man who supposedly lived simply, on a laborer's salary, having such an expensive, brand new vehicle.

Then I realized that Abbott was probably like lots of guys I'd known over the years, especially single ones, who lived as modestly as possible in order to spend every extra cent they had on their vehicles.

Something about everything around me didn't square with the notion of a man who would lash out and brutally murder a man in cold blood, let alone cunningly frame someone else for the crime. I could easily see Abbott getting a bit too tight at a local watering hole and ending up in a fight. Possibly losing his temper standing in line at the grocery store and lashing out verbally.

But to purposely set out to do someone in? Not to mention being conniving enough to frame another for it? It just didn't sit with the image I had of the man, and I wondered if Thayer and his lawyer were merely grasping at straws.

Even so, I went about exploring the small garage.

Didn't take long. Abbott, despite his occupation, didn't seem to be much of a handy man. He had a small shelf full of ordinary tools, nothing you wouldn't find at any small hardware store. No special, deluxe, ultra-super set of every size wrench, hammer and screwdriver known to man. No cordless ten tools in one setup. Not even, as far as I could see, a socket wrench.

A small pile of two by fours, about a foot high, occupied one corner of the garage, and a broken-down, obsolete, and half-rusted refrigerator canted over in the other corner.

Amid the squalor and disrepair of it all, the pickup stood out like a diamond. I couldn't imagine that anyone who took such good care of a vehicle would have it less than pristine on the inside, but a thorough search was a thorough search.

Tucked away in the garage as it was, Abbott had left the truck unlocked. I opened the driver's door and took a good look around the front seat. Granted, I only did an eyeball inspection, but the interior looked as well-cared for as the exterior.

Then I levered the front driver's seat down, to take a good look at the rear of the cab, and saw it.

It was faint, and if I hadn't been specifically looking for something incriminating I would have missed it, but I hadn't and I didn't.

I took out my flashlight, snapped it on and angled the beam down for a closer look, almost hoping that a wider expanse of light would reveal my initial identification had been faulty.

Nope.

And as I stood there staring at the back bottom of the driver's seat, down at the very bottom edge, I could tell that my first hunch had been on the spot.

A thin, almost microscopically slender, trickle of dried blood traced its way from one side of the seat to the other.

CHAPTER THIRTY-NINE

TWO DAYS LATER, AROUND THREE IN THE AFTERNOON, Josh Nichols stopped by the gym. He didn't knock, but walked right into my office and took a seat in one of my client chairs.

I got up, went over to the coffee maker, raised the pot in his direction. He nodded, still without a word, and I poured a couple of cups black. I walked back over to my desk, handed him his cup, then sat down.

Nichols took a long, slow drink, then leaned back and stared at the ceiling for about a minute or so. After he'd seen whatever he needed to see in my plain white spackle, he lowered his gaze to me.

"Your guy's off the hook," he said, "being released as we speak."

"By my guy, I assume you mean Felix Thayer?"

"How many people you been working for that are under arrest lately?"

"Far as I know, only Thayer."

"Then that's the one. Turns out he may be a world-class prick, but he's not a murderer."

"Oh?" I gave him an inquisitive look, glad for all those years I'd spent acting in the wrestling ring. And if you don't think pro wrestlers are world class actors, you need to think again.

"Oh," Nichols said. "We got a tip, anonymous phone call, believe it or not, that said we needed to check out one of the janitors at the university."

"Sounds like a crank," I said, "besides, you've already got your guy in custody."

"True. But the lieutenant, despite his big city pedigree, or maybe because of it, is pretty much by the book. So we began checking things out."

"And?"

Nichols gave me one of his patented hard, searching cop looks. I thought about making faces at him, but decided to stay poker faced.

"And when we started digging around, took us no time at all to come up with enough probable cause to get a search warrant for his place."

"So fast?"

"I'm telling you, buddy. His alibi didn't hold up; he got evasive under questioning; we found some stuff written down in his locker at work about how much he hated Hartness. It was crazy how much stuff we found."

I nodded, trying to look interested and surprised at the same time.

"Then there was the blood," Nichols said.

"Blood?"

"Yep. Turns out this hourly employee at the school has two vehicles, a daily driver that's a beaten-up old Camry and a brand-new F-350, still as clean and shiny as the day it drove off the lot."

"Yeah?"

"Yeah. Except for a little smear of blood on the back of the driver's seat. Blood that turns out to be the same type as Michael Hartness."

"Really?" I thought about doing the raised-eyebrow thing, but figured that would go a little overboard. "DNA?"

Nichols shook his head. "Too soon yet. It'll be several weeks before that gets back, but there was enough to make us interrogate Abbott, and that Lancaster fellow got wind of it and started making motions. Before you know it, Thayer's out of the clink and off to freedom."

"All's well," I said.

Nichols stared at me for a second. I noticed he hadn't yet drunk any of his coffee.

"I almost expected to come over here and find you getting dressed for the victory party. You telling me you knew nothing about this?"

I shook my head. "I was fired. Remember? I've been off the case."

"Uh huh. Then you wouldn't know anything about who could have gotten into Abbott's house, probably done an illegal search, and left us a tip about checking out the man's truck for blood?"

"I'm telling you, it's all news to me. Sounds like it all worked out for the best, though."

"Not really."

I blinked at that. "How so?"

He took a long drink, draining nearly half the cup in one swallow before putting it down on my desk. "Gut hunch," he said.

"Say what?"

"It looks too pat, too easy. If I had to ignore the evidence and go with my gut. I'd still say Thayer's the one who killed him."

I took in a slow sip of breath. Nichols was nobody's fool as a cop, and I'd take his gut over a mountain of evidence any day.

"But I'm guessing with all this new evidence . . ."

"Right. We didn't have any choice but to bring Abbott in and let your guy go. Where do we go from here?"

Obviously, Nichols didn't have a clue.

The problem was, neither did I.

CHAPTER FORTY

After Nichols left, I tried to focus on paperwork, but couldn't concentrate. I wandered around The Blaster for a while, checking on clients, stopping to talk to a few old-timers here and there, but it didn't take long to realize I was just spinning my wheels. I was practically bouncing off the walls with a combination of energy, frustration and confusion and needed some way to release it all.

At one point I stood in a corner, deliberately ignoring Keri Eckland's questioning look, and surveyed my little slice of empire.

Thanks to Lisa Nolan's wheedling, pleading and conniving, over the last few years the place has darned near gentrified until it practically gleams with the most modern assortment of bikes, resistance machines, treadmills and anything else you could imagine could be used to tone the body.

However, there was one piece of equipment we didn't own, and it occurred to me that that was what I needed.

I went into my office for a change of clothes, said goodbye to Keri, and headed out. A short drive took me to a slightly run-down strip mall on the far south side of town, one that straddled a low-income housing development and a residential neighborhood.

The establishment at the north end of the strip mall didn't have a sign proclaiming its existence, and it didn't have any sort of decoration. The front was merely two large blacked-out floor to ceiling windows and an old, scarred wooden door.

An ordinary passerby would walk or drive right by the place and assume it used to house some store or other type business, maybe a bakery, that had gone by the wayside.

I tried the knob, and it was unlocked. You never know ahead of time, because Lonny doesn't keep any sort of regular hours. Walking inside, I was greeted by total emptiness in an old, waterfront-type boxing gym.

I spent my athletic prime in pro-wrestling, but along the way I crossed paths every now and then with boxers. Lonny Walker was an old school boxing coach who spent most of his life and career shuttling between Providence and St. Louis. When in Lonny's presence, you couldn't help but think of the old Rocky movies because he combines the physique of an older, graying Apollo Creed with the personality and cantankerousness of Rocky's coach, Micky.

Although the place appeared empty, I assumed someone lurked in the back. Enough people who frequented the place knew me that I wasn't concerned about being hassled, and within a couple of minutes I was gloved up and banging away on a heavy bag.

As I pummeled the bag, I ran my mind through everything that had gone on in the couple of weeks since Susan Thayer had come calling.

It didn't feel right, but then again it hadn't felt right from the beginning. Officially, the cops were close to proving George Abbott as the killer, and while it all added up evidence-wise, naturally the DA's focus, none of it added up gutwise, at least not for me.

Then again, what did that matter to me? As far as I could see, my involvement in the affair was over, had basically wrapped with my anonymous call to the cops that sicced them onto Abbott. There were, however, a couple of niggling little questions that wouldn't leave me alone.

One, if Abbott were the killer, what did he have against Hartness? From our one conversation, I assumed he liked the guy. Abbott at least spoke warmer of him than he did Thayer. Of course, if most people killed someone they wouldn't turn around and badmouth them to an investigator, so that didn't prove a whole lot.

And why go to the trouble of framing Thayer? It could possibly come out that Abbott had an issue with both men and wanted to pull some sort of double whammy, but the whole thing still seemed extravagantly complex. Outside of a cheap novel, who would go to that much trouble just to rid themselves of some irritation?

More than that, though, the question of the mob and its involvement still loomed. It seemed like every time during this case I turned around I was tripping over either Sean or some of his goons, and I still had no reasonable explanation for their presence.

And if my discussion with Nichols the day before had been any indication, the cops themselves weren't too happy with how things were shaking out, even though every step of the way they'd followed where the evidence led them. But they had other business to keep track of and other cases to follow, so while it bothered them, they couldn't exactly spend a whole lot of time worrying over stuff they couldn't control.

I, on the other hand, at the moment had nothing but time on my hands.

After several minutes of pounding away, I realized that I needed to do this kind of thing more often. My arms had already begun to burn, and the sweatshirt I'd donned before leaving the Blaster was soaked through and dripping onto the floor. My heart rate had increased, but probably by more than I wanted it to.

Then there was the question of the university itself. I couldn't know for sure without talking to anyone, but my guess was that few people would be all that happy if Thayer returned to work. It was pretty obvious by now that if he'd been the actual guilty party the whole department chair thing wouldn't have been his motivation, but the fact of his wife's affair with Hartness.

A door somewhere in the back opened up, and one of Lonny's workers, a young guy in his teens, came out and began wiping down equipment. Seeing me pounding away on the bag, he gave a quick nod, a simple signal of recognition that he'd seen me. I was pretty sure, the way I was dripping, blowing and pounding, that he didn't expect any reply.

What the DA now had was a man who had the oldest conceivable motive for murder who seemed by all counts to be innocent, and a guy with no obvious motive who the evidence showed as guilty. None of that made any sense.

And again, what the hell did Sean O'Flaherty have to do with it? And how did he get on to my working on the case so quick? His thugs were trailing me literally the day I began working for Susan Thayer. How the hell did that all connect?

My legs went from rubber to jelly. I lowered my arms and took a step back. My entire upper body felt on fire, most noticeably my lungs, and I realized I should have marked when I started. By my best guess, I'd been pounding away for something like thirty minutes, and looking at it one way it had been a waste of time.

I hadn't solved the mystery, and I hadn't been able to connect the dots. But there was one thing I knew for sure.

I couldn't let it go just yet.

CHAPTER FORTY-ONE

FOUR O'CLOCK THE NEXT AFTERNOON, I was sitting in the visitor's room at the jail with George Abbott across from me.

"What do you want?" Abbott practically snarled into the phone.

"Wanted to talk to you."

"About what? Don't you think I figured out you're the reason I'm in here?"

"They did find some evidence, you know."

"Planted."

I shook my head to unkink some of my frustration. "Think about it a minute, Abbott. Why would someone plant evidence against someone like you?"

"You think about it, dude. You saw my truck, right? No, that's okay. Don't bother to say one way or the other. We both know you got inside my place. Which means you probably saw the blood on the seatback, right?"

I gave him the most neutral look I could come up with.

"Like I said," he continued, "you don't need to say anything one way or the other. This is all I've got to ask you. Would someone who took care of a vehicle the way I took care of that truck take it out on a night he was going to murder someone? Especially when he had a piece of shit Camry sitting right there leaking oil in the driveway? If nothing else, which one would be more noticeable leaving a crime scene? "

"If the blood was planted, how could it have been done?"

"You kidding? I thought you were supposed to be some kind of professional at this stuff. I work from four to midnight, six days a week. How hard would it be for someone to figure out my schedule?"

Not hard, as it turned out. It had only taken me a day and a half to get his routine down pat.

Far as that went, his house wasn't exactly the most burglar-proof I'd ever seen.

"You'd better fix this, mister," Abbott said.

"Come again?"

"You don't get it, do you? You've been played every step of the way. Thayer's as guilty as they come. He used you to get him out and me in. Who the hell knows what he's going to do next?"

I didn't have an answer to that, either.

But I had an idea of someone who might.

CHAPTER FORTY-TWO

The first time around, Daniel Lancaster had visited my place of business, so it only seemed appropriate to return the favor.

His office space wasn't swanky or flashy, but it also wasn't the kind of bare-bones, storefront operation you'd expect a struggling young lawyer to have. He had a modest space in one of the smaller buildings at the western edge of downtown, sandwiched between an insurance office and a financial advisor's.

The office was a small affair, one outer room with a door on the right that had a small brass plate with Lancaster's name on it. Maybe a bit of an ego stretch there, as there were no other names on the front of the door and no other doors in the room, but cut the guy some slack.

At least he didn't have a cheap-looking championship belt hanging over his desk.

The outer room held a couple of black leather easy chairs, a dark brown coffee table with a few magazines scattered on it, and a brass floor lamp in the corner.

It also had a woman, mid-forties and blonde, sitting behind a metal-rimmed desk toward the back. She was tapping at a computer and looked up as I approached.

"Can I help you?"

"Mr. Lancaster, please."

She gave me a bit of a frown and glanced down at a small yellow notepad next to her computer. "Is he expecting you?"

"Darned if I know," I said, giving her the warmest grin I could muster, "but I think he'll see me."

The frown deepened, though not all that much, as she picked up the handset to her desk phone. "Name?"

"Sam Quinton."

"Are you looking to retain his services, Mr. Quinton?"

"Does Mr. Lancaster handle civil litigation at all?"

"No, only criminal matters," she said.

"So why would you think I need a lawyer?"

"Well," she drawled the syllable out as her gaze roamed up and down my length.

Maybe it was my longish, graying hair.

Or the jeans, tee-shirt and leather jacket I wore.

Or the fact that I hadn't shaved in a couple of days.

It occurred to me that if she thought I was a potential client, instead of a bill collector or process server, she'd let me in to see the man quicker.

I put a deliberate sneer on my face. "Tell you what, missy. Why don't you just buzz your boss and tell him I'm here, and let him take it from there? Then you can get back to your filing, or whatever the hell it is that you do."

She lowered the phone down to the desk. "Don't get tough with me buster. The trainer at the gym I go to's been teaching me kick boxing."

She was obviously tougher than I'd expected. Maybe I should start offering pro wrestling classes at my gym. An hour of teaching you false moves at sixty bucks a pop.

Nah, Lisa would go ballistic on me if I even suggested it.

I was trying to come up with another witty line to break our obvious impasse when the door on the right side of the room opened up, and Lancaster looked out at me.

"Quinton."

I nodded. The guy looked horrible.

"I guess we have to talk," he said.

"I guess so," I said.

With his right hand, he ushered me into his office.

The kid's eyes were red-rimmed, and he hadn't shaved in a couple of days.

I go unshaven too, but on me it looks manly and tough. At least, that's what I tell myself. Josh Nichols told me once it makes me look like an over-the-hill punk rocker.

Lancaster's hair was scattered every which way, and he had a hard time looking me in the eye.

"What can I do for you, Quinton?"

"Let's forget that for a minute. What the hell's wrong with you?"

He glanced my way for a second before looking away again. "Seriously? You come to my office and ask me what's wrong? Tell me what you want and get out, okay?"

Instead of answering, I slouched down in my chair, crossed my arms and stretched my legs out in front of me. I stayed that way for only about half a minute before the kid broke.

"Oh, fuck," he said, slumping down behind his desk. "You know why I became a lawyer?"

"To make money?" I suggested.

He nodded, still not quite looking at me. "That's right. To make money. To provide a nice life for myself and, someday, for my future family."

"But?"

He tapped his fingers on the desk a couple of times before slouching even further back, craning his neck so he was almost looking at the ceiling. "But I basically want to do the right thing. Give my clients good advice and defense, make sure things run like they're supposed to run. You know, all that rah rah glory stuff they talk about in first year law school."

"So what's bugging you?" I asked.

He levered himself up, straightening so that he could look me straight on. "What do you think's bothering me?"

"If I had to guess, I'd say you're facing the possibility that you helped get a guilty man out of jail and put an innocent man in his place."

"Hole in one," Lancaster said as he placed his palms flat on his desk. "And I'm guessing you're here for pretty much the same reason."

I squirmed in my chair. "Yeah," I said, "you could say that. It seemed like an obvious move on my part at the time, but looking back on it—"

Lancaster nodded. "Then what do we do about it?"

Now it was my turn to look away, but I forced myself not to.

I met the guy eye to eye.

"Damned if I know," I said.

About that time my phone rang. I pulled it out of my pocket, checked to see who was calling and, at seeing Josh Nichols's name, figured I should take it.

"Excuse me," I said to Lancaster, "cops."

The lawyer nodded as I punched up the call.

"Yeah, Josh," I said.

"Blondie, you busy at the moment?"

I glanced at Lancaster. "Not really. Just consulting on some business with an attorney I know. What's up?"

He gave me the name of a state park to the south of town. "Why don't you come out here, buddy? Got something the lieutenant wants you to see."

CHAPTER FORTY-THREE

"WOULDN'T BOTHER ME AT ALL if you felt responsible for this," Santiago said when I arrived at the scene.

A weekend hiker had found the corpse while it was still fairly fresh. Stony Creek Park, a densely-wooded area just to the south of Providence, sprawls over several acres and provides all sorts of trails, small cliffs to scale and horseback riding opportunities. It's a mecca for nature lovers around the area.

Though it now appeared as if someone had considered it appealing for another type of activity as well.

Nichols must have given my name to the uniforms manning the perimeter because I was let in without any problem. As I approached the flurry of activity, all centered around a common point, I knew in general what waited for me, but not any particulars.

Thus, as I came abreast of the suits, the lieutenant's comment puzzled me at first. I could see the body was female, fairly badly battered, and even to my inexpert eye it appeared as if the back of her head was bashed in.

"What do you mean? Responsible in what way?"

Nichols squirmed, as if he'd been caught cheating on a math test, while Santiago mainly gave me the umpteenth version of the glare I got from him practically anytime we came together. Then he knelt down and, his hands encased in clear gloves, turned the corpse over on its back.

The sightless eyes of Susan Thayer stared up at me.

"Dammit," I muttered.

"You got any ideas about who did this?" Santiago asked.

Someone had really done a number on the pretty lady. Her face smashed in, blue marks around her throat, and two rivers of dried blood running down from somewhere in that mass of once-shiny black hair, now itself looking dull and lifeless.

And after all that, the bastard had dumped her in the woods to be preyed on by any animals who came along.

"I asked you a question, Quinton."

"Yes, Lieutenant," I said without taking my eyes off the body. "I've got an idea, and it's probably the same idea you have."

"Would have saved everyone a lot of trouble if you hadn't helped spring him."

I clenched my fists rather than respond to the man, mainly because I agreed with him. "You got anything to go on?" I asked.

"Depends on your expectations," Santiago said. "After all, none of us are hot-ass private eyes who get their kicks out of making the local fuzz look like yokels."

"Can it, Lieutenant." I finally tore my gaze from the woman and looked over at the cop. "I found evidence, and I turned it over to you. You guys followed what I gave you and figured you arrested the wrong man and let him go. The fact that he got out of jail and turned around to get even with his wife has nothing to do with me."

"Unless you got it wrong, hot shot."

"Meaning?"

"Meaning what if we had the right guy all along? After all, he had one hell of a motive to do in both Hartness and his wife."

I considered pointing out to Santiago that he hadn't been all that angry at me when I'd supplied the initial motive to add to the case against Felix Thayer, but as I watched him standing over the body, I decided to let it go.

In the year or so since Santiago had arrived in Providence, we'd only had a couple of run-ins, so I didn't know him all that well. Even so, the man was a mystery.

From his polished, big-city manners, to his tailored suits that no cop lower than a chief should have been able to afford, to the

Jaguar I'd heard he drove, everything about the man screamed "corrupt cop." Yet his predecessor had been genuinely corrupt, and I found it hard to believe that even our city council would okay the hiring of another obvious crook to fill the slot.

Yet as the three of us stood there on the edge of the wooded park, circled around Susan Thayer's violated body, the guy who seemed to have walked right out of a *Godfather* script looked almost on the point of tears.

"I followed the evidence, Lieutenant," I said, even as I spoke realizing how lame it sounded. "Same as you guys did."

"Then why don't you follow it right the hell on out of here private eye. Beat it, and let some real cops try to untangle the mess you caused."

That last bit of antagonism was a bit much, and I started to bite something back in reply. But Nichols caught my eye and shook his head. Bowing to someone with greater common sense than myself, I turned and headed back through the layers of police presence, back to my Cherokee to get the hell out of there.

And I knew right where I was going next.

CHAPTER FORTY-FOUR

I found Thayer in the first place I tried and the last place most people would expect. Finding him so quick wasn't really a matter of getting lucky. By this time, I knew Dr. Felix Thayer more than I would ever want to, and his location so shortly after his wife's death made perfect sense.

In short, I found him in his office at the university.

With Felicia Adams not at her counter in the front part of the office suite, there was no one to stop me as I walked around the counter and straight toward Thayer's office. The door was shut, but motion I could see through the small window indicated he had someone in there with him.

Student? Colleague? Another poor soul he was setting up for the kill?

Who knew?

Who gave a damn?

The door wasn't locked, unfortunately depriving me of the sheer pleasure of smashing my way in. I settled for swiftly throwing the panel open and barging in, harkening back to my ring days to present the darkest, most terrifying facial expression I could put on.

Turned out Thayer's visitor was a young male, around nineteen or so. No doubt a student.

Today would probably go down in his memory as the scariest day of his college career.

Thayer jumped up when I barged in, his hands clutching the edge of his desk. He looked wildly around for a second, as if searching for some way out of the enclosed office.

I growled at him once, then turned and pinned my gaze on the young man still rooted to his chair.

"Out!" I snarled, and the kid found his legs and went up and out.

"What do you want?" Thayer hissed, though his voice cracked a bit.

"I just came from the park," I said.

"I don't know what—"

Taking two strides forward, I slammed my hand flat on his desk, the crack almost reverberating. Thayer blanched and stumbled back, flat against the wall behind him.

"You pathetic bastard." I did my own hiss, but mine was much more menacing than his. "Do you get off by screwing around with people's lives?"

He tried to shrink even further into the wall, something he quickly found impossible to do. "You—you get out of here. You've got no business being—"

One sideways move took me around the desk and up into his face. In my peripheral vision, I saw the outer suite still empty. I placed my right hand against the wall, almost leaning into it, and with my left I grasped Thayer's jaw and neck, then banged him up against the wall.

Not hard. Not nearly as hard as guys used to bang me in the ring, but for a civilian college professor, it probably felt like the smack of doom.

His teeth clanked together, and I'm not sure but I think he may have broken one or two. Gripping his neck and jaw tighter, I lifted him a couple of inches off the floor and leaned in till barely a millimeter existed between us.

"I'm going to get you, Thayer. You've got two people killed and one rotting in jail. Somehow or other, you're responsible for it all, and I'm going to make sure it all comes crashing down on you."

Before the poor sap could answer, a male voice called out from the doorway.

"Hold it right there, mister!"

I half turned, still not letting go of the professor, and saw two campus police, a young man and woman, standing in the door with their nightsticks drawn.

The scared kid must have barely gotten out of his professor's office before calling security.

"Let the man go," the woman cop said, "and hold up those hands."

I smiled, a sincere smile to show I wasn't all that much of a threat, and eased my grip on Thayer. Scrambling free, he huddled in the corner, crouched down, and pointed at me.

"Get him out of here! He tried to kill me. If you hadn't come—"

I turned to the professor again. "But they did come, Felix. And it's damned good for you that they did."

"That's enough, mister," the male cop again. "Back away, raise up those hands and turn your back to us."

I thought about asking if they could chalk the whole thing up to overexuberance on my part, but one look at the grim set of their faces indicated otherwise.

Doing as they requested, in another moment I was up against the wall, spread-eagled in the standard position, with Thayer behind me screaming about all the charges he was going to bring.

About thirty seconds into that, right before they trundled me away, the young female cop turned back to him.

"Shut up," she said, "sir."

CHAPTER FORTY-FIVE

"NEXT TIME, REMIND ME TO PICK BETTER FRIENDS," Josh Nichols said about four hours later.

I tried to think of something to say to lighten the mood, but not a darned thing came to mind. When they'd booked me into the city jail, I immediately thought of calling Bernie Lyman. On second consideration, I reached out to Nichols.

Bernie could get me out by going through the legal process, which even at its speediest would take time. I hoped that Nichols could throw his weight around a little and find a shortcut.

Took him a while, but the guy came through.

"They don't want you anywhere around the university ever again," he said as we stopped by the front desk to get my personal effects. As they were handed over, I began stuffing wallet, keys, cell phone and cash into my pockets. I toyed with making a big deal out of counting out the cash to make sure it was all there, but the grimness of Nichols's face changed my mind.

"Who's they?" I asked as I signed the last few forms to get the hell out of there.

"Who do you think? The university police force."

"They don't have the authority to order someone to stay away."

"They do if the order comes from the chancellor."

"I guess my budding friendship with him has hit a rocky patch."

Once I had everything back in my pockets where it belonged, Nichols motioned with his head and I followed him outside. We exited the central doors of the station and walked to the end of the block.

"What's the latest on Abbott?" I asked.

"Still inside. Where he's staying, far as it seems. At arraignment he wasn't granted any bail, so that's that."

"Come on, Josh. You and I both know he didn't do it."

"Of course, we do. Same with the lieutenant and anyone at all familiar with the case. But as is often the problem in my job, buddy, knowing and proving are two different things."

I frowned. "Even if you can't pin the Hartness murder on Thayer, anything at all on his wife?"

"Remember that we had that sleety rain the other night?"

I groaned. "You telling me any good physical evidence washed away?"

"Far as we can tell so far. There may be some trace evidence, but nothing anyone's come up with yet."

"You manage to search their house?"

"Yep, and didn't his new lawyer scream about that. Called us all kinds of names and threatened all sorts of legal mumbo jumbo."

"New lawyer? He dumped Lancaster?"

"Way I heard it Lancaster dumped him. Wants nothing more to do with the guy. Can't say as I blame him."

"But the bottom line is that the victim's house was a legitimate object of a search."

"Correct."

"Yet you struck out."

"Of course, we did. You think someone with Thayer's brains is going to leave any evidence lying around."

"Not unless it's evidence he wants you to find," I said, and both of us went silent for a minute.

"Problem is," Nichols finally continued, "that the DA has at least one murder neatly wrapped up and tied in a bundle for him, and he's not about to worry about any dangling threads. Especially since we made him look like a goof when we, his words, jumped the gun and arrested Thayer."

"Dangling threads such as the actual killer set the poor sap up to take the fall for him?"

"Exactly. At the moment, with the investigation officially closed, there's not much Santiago, myself, or anyone else can do about it."

"Officially," I said.

"That's right."

For the first time since we left the station, I turned and looked squarely at my friend.

"What about doing something unofficially?" I asked.

Nichols shook his head. "I wouldn't know anything about that."

"Uh huh."

"Far as that goes," he said with a light grin, "I wouldn't want to know."

"Good to know," I said before turning and walking away.

CHAPTER FORTY-SIX

I MET TALIA SANDERSON AT THE LOCAL outpost of a well-known restaurant chain that specializes in old-time, Southern cooking. When I'd called and asked if we could get together, she'd looked at her calendar, claimed she had a faculty meeting at 4:30 but could be free by six, and asked if we could get together then.

Meeting up at the home-style cooking place had been her idea. "I'm famished," she'd said over the phone, "haven't had a thing since a cup of yogurt for breakfast. You wouldn't mind treating me to a full-spread meal, would you?"

"Not at all," I'd said.

A few minutes later we were seated with menus in hand and drinks in front of us. I guessed that Talia had come straight from her meeting because she was still wearing the skirt, blouse and wool jacket that I'd imagined she'd worn to work in the morning. She looked a little drawn around the eyes.

"Rough day?" I asked, merely to start the conversation going as we examined our menus.

"I've had better," she said, "but I've also had worse."

"What was your meeting about?"

She gave me a hooded look. "I would think someone in your profession would understand the idea of confidentiality and closed doors."

"Which means what you talked about was super hush hush?" I said.

Talia nodded. "You could say that."

"Chancellor Withers there?"

"All the movers and shakers were, including a couple of folks from the state capital. One of the few times that as a dean I felt like a lowly employee."

About that time our food came, surprising me a bit because usually this place took half an hour or so. The server plunked our plates down, asked if we needed anything else and, once we said everything looked great, moved on to another table.

"As long as we're on the subject of university doings," Talia said. "There's a story going around about a large, fearsome looking man who assaulted Felix Thayer in his office earlier today."

"Have you also heard the story about Susan Thayer's dead body being found outside of town?" I asked as I speared a manly portion of mac n' cheese with my fork.

"As a matter of fact, we did."

"We?" I looked up. "I'm guessing that I can figure out what your meeting was about."

Talia stared at her food for a moment, then sighed, slumped her shoulders and pushed her plate away.

"Fuck," she whispered.

I positioned my elbows on the table and rested my chin in my hands. "Tell me about it."

Her face tightened, but at least she looked me in the eyes. "We want that man out of the university. He's a friggin' cancer. But we can't budge him."

"Because?"

"Because it would look awful. As far as being a professor, his tenure protects him."

"I thought if you were involved in something criminal that went by the wayside."

Talia nodded, but the move didn't have much oomph behind it. "It would. But he was exonerated, mainly because a certain private detective I know found evidence that another person did the crime."

I grimaced, but couldn't disagree. The fact that I was certain by now that I'd been hoodwinked, that Thayer had somehow led me to find the evidence to get him off, didn't matter.

"Don't remind me," I said. "George Abbott's still in jail for something he didn't do."

"He is?" Incredulity made her voice go up about half an octave. Before I could answer, our young waitress scurried over to see if anything was wrong.

"No," Talia said. "No problem."

The girl's eyes strayed to our plates, both of which had barely been touched. "Are you sure?" she said. "If something's wrong with the food—"

"Not at all." I smiled as I spoke. "We've both had bad days at work and we're comparing notes."

Talia nodded in agreement, and the young girl moved away, though she didn't really look as if she believed us.

"You didn't get him out of jail?" Talia hissed, giving me a look that, if I hadn't been such a tough old war horse, would have had me slithering under the table.

"There's no obvious way to, even though I'm convinced he's innocent. Same with the cops"

"But you have no proof."

"That's right. And unfortunately, it's a high-profile case, and without any actual proof of his innocence, the district attorney plans on keeping Abbott in jail until something better comes along."

"The decision's been made to make Thayer department chair," Talia said.

I felt as if someone had come along and punched me in the gut. "You guys are going to promote a two-time murderer?"

Talia's face hardened even more. "But he's not being charged with anything, remember? And if we denied him based on anything like that, he'd have a helluva lawsuit against us. Even that rookie representing him could take us to the cleaners."

Although I hated her logic, I had to agree with her. Thayer had worked everything out perfectly on his side.

"He's untouchable," I said.

Talia nodded. "Absolutely. Our meeting was so long because we were looking for alternatives. Any way to get him out of his job and off campus. Especially after he murdered his wife."

"For which there's no evidence either," I said.

The two of us stared at each other for a moment. Out of the corner of my eye I saw our waitress hovering, as if wondering whether to bother us again, and I realized that neither of us had yet eaten from our plates.

I turned her way and smiled, doing my best to nonverbally assure her we were fine.

When I turned back to Talia, she was giving me an intense look.

"What?" I said.

She frowned, as if deciding something. "I'm going to take a chance on trusting you."

"Worse chances to take," I said.

She glanced around us, almost like a character out of a spy movie. "I'm about to violate university policy," she said, "and about half a dozen government regulations. But I don't know what else to do."

I held my breath for a minute before nodding. "Okay."

Another minute or so went by while Talia stared down at her hands. When she finally began talking, she spoke to the tabletop rather than to me.

"Two months ago, we gave Felix his notice. He was supposed to be gone at the end of next year."

"Notice?" I said. "I thought he couldn't be fired."

She shook her head, still unable to face me. I guessed that this was one of the few times in her life, if not the very first, that she'd deliberately violated any kind of confidentiality. "Ordinarily, yes. Professors with tenure have almost complete job security."

"Almost," I said.

She nodded and after a second managed to bring herself to face me again. "Thayer's been a problem for years. You no doubt came across lots of examples. Chancellor Withers has been looking for some legitimate way to get him gone. Jacob Wind?"

"The graduate student who killed himself last year."

Talia nodded. "That was the final straw for us. We came across information, unofficially, that Felix had tormented the young man, practically making him slave away doing menial tasks and at the same time belitting the boy's work."

"All unofficial. Nothing on record," I said.

"True," she said, "but we managed to add it to everything else in his file and make enough of a case to give him his notice."

"If that's true, why not fire him and get it done with?'

"It's customary to give someone a year's grace period, allow them to find work and leave with a little dignity."

Something clicked in my head. "A year," I said.

"Uh huh."

"Which if he would have become department chair—"

"Would have made it that much easier for him to move on."

"But now—"

"Now, to the public he appears to be a wrongly accused man who barely managed to avoid a murder conviction."

"Kind of tough to fire a guy in those circumstances," I said.

"What's left to do?" Talia finally broke the silence.

An idea popped into my head. Something so outrageous that I almost discounted it before it was fully formed.

But I didn't toss it. Not right away.

"Sgt. Nichols and I were talking earlier, and he suggested that, at the moment at least, there's no way to officially touch Felix."

"And so?" Talia asked. "Is there any other way to get him?"

"Actually," I said, "I may have just thought of one."

CHAPTER FORTY-SEVEN

THIS TIME, O'FLAHERTY AND I MET ON NEUTRAL GROUND.

The day after dinner with Talia, I spent about five or six hours dropping as many hints, signals, clues and indicators as I could in every nook and cranny of Providence, and the surrounding area of Carson County, where I figured the slightest chance that O'Flaherty would get the word.

Shortly after two, halfway through a BLT from a local sub shop that, as an out-of-town friend had once informed me, rivaled anything to be found in New York, my cell phone rang.

The screen indicated an unknown number, which amped up my hopes that this was the call I'd been waiting for. It was almost too much to hope that the person on the other end was O'Flaherty himself, but seeing as how nothing had gone in a straight line on this case one could always hope.

"Quinton?"

So much for idle hopes. Whoever it was, the gravelly voice on the other end definitely didn't sound like O'Flaherty's.

Not unless he was a master at disguising his voice.

"Yeah?" I said.

"Word is you want to get together with someone."

"Word is right."

"What about?"

"That's between Sean and me," I said.

"Maybe he don't want to talk to you," Gravel Voice replied.

"Why don't you find out and get back to me? I'm guessing all you have to do is turn to the side, so it shouldn't take long. While you're at it, tell Sean it's Susan I want to talk about."

"Hold on."

About two minutes went by before Gravel Voice came back on. "Okay," he said. "Here's how it's going to go."

He proceeded to name a place and time. I pondered pushing back with my own meeting place, so as not to appear too wussy, but decided there was no point in possibly spoiling the whole deal.

Firmly ensconced in its position as the most progressively liberal city in Missouri, Providence has, per capita, more than its fair share of vegan/keto-based/natural food eateries. The one Gravel Voice had specified was a little place a couple of blocks off Main Street that only held about ten tables.

He'd set the meeting at four that afternoon, leading me to naturally show up about three o'clock and park my Cherokee in the lot of a pharmacy about two blocks down from the diner, positioned in such a way that, save for the occasional traffic flying by, I could entirely see the front and east side of the small, red-board building.

I could only partially see the west side, but that was bordered by a chain link fence that portioned off the parking for a finance company.

The rear of the building I couldn't see at all, but you take what you can get.

I figured if O'Flaherty planned any kind of sneak attack or double cross, though why he'd think it necessary to do so I had no idea, arriving half an hour early would make it more likely that I'd catch any sneakiness in action. With that in mind, I'd doubled the time, thus ensuring that there'd be no way for Sean or his men to sneak up on me.

In my side view mirrors, I saw two black SUV's pull up in each of the parking slots alongside me. The rear doors on my side opened, and one man got out of each of the vehicles.

So much for strategic thinking.

The men didn't advance. Instead, they hung back a few feet, their gazes roving everywhere but at me. After a couple of minutes of that, while I sat as calmly as I could, the front passenger door of the SUV on my opposite side opened up, and O'Flaherty got out. He nodded to the two men, opened the door, and climbed into my car.

I worked at controlling my breathing as the top mobster in the central part of the state settled down into the seat.

"You planning something fancy, Quinton?" he asked.

"Yeah," I said. "Making sure you didn't pull some slick move."

"Looks like I outslicked you."

I nodded but didn't reply. When you've got nothing to say, you've got nothing to say.

"I've known about you for a while now," the mob boss continued. "Paddy used to talk good about you quite a bit. Since I settled down in this area, we haven't had any sort of interaction, and now in the last few weeks I keep bumping into you."

"Some people are just lucky."

"Maybe, maybe not. But you've definitely got balls to meet me like this, so why don't you get to it. What are you here about?"

"Not what, who."

"Okay, then who?"

"Susan Thayer."

O'Flaherty paused a minute, and his face clinched up.

"What about whoever you said?"

"Come on, Sean. You think I went to this trouble to get face to face with you without knowing the score. Your interest in all this was because of Susan Thayer."

"What makes you think that?"

I slumped my shoulders in as theatrical a manner as I could. "I spent a lot of time on the computer last night, Sean. Granted, I'm not a tech whiz or anything, but these days someone in my field has to at least know the basics of how to search for someone. How do you think most bail jumpers are caught nowadays? After I was through on the machine, I made quite a few phone calls back east."

"To whom?"

"You think I'm going to tell you? Why don't we leave it at I got the whole story and wrap this up."

Now it was O'Flaherty's turn to relax. He sank into the seat, and his face loosened up.

"Paddy always said you were good. And with everything my boys have reported back, I've got the feeling you tried to do right by her."

"If so, I wasn't very successful."

For the first time, O'Flaherty turned and looked my way. His eyes showed a swirling combination of anger, grief and frustration. "No, you weren't. But I didn't do a whole lot better."

"I'm guessing you tried, though."

"How'd you manage to put this together?" O'Flaherty asked. "What got you started down this road?"

"Eliminating possibilities," I said. "I've been wondering all along two things. What was your interest in all this, and how did you glom onto so fast the fact that I was involved. Then it hit me."

"Yeah?"

"Yeah," I mimicked. "You were keeping an eye on Susan, and her coming to me is what got you looking my way."

"Like I said, Paddy always said you were smart."

"But one thing's had me kind of puzzled," I said.

"What?"

"You know who killed her, right?"

"Of course. That no good scumbag husband of hers. I know it in my gut. Even if the cartoon cops in this town can't seem to do anything about it."

"Right. Which has me wondering why you haven't done anything about the situation."

The gangster took a long, deep breath. I wondered for a second if I was pushing things too much, but figured I'd gone too far down the road to turn back now.

Besides, with his men standing right outside I was kind of trapped.

"What do you expect me to do?" he finally asked.

"Well, as a starter, I'm wondering why Thayer's still walking around breathing. I would have expected him to be room temperature by now."

That swirl of emotion in O'Flaherty's eyes intensified, and I had the feeling I was looking at a predator doing everything possible to hold himself back from striking.

"Maybe you're not as smart as you think you are, Quinton."

"That's a possibility. But a more likely possibility is that something's preventing you from taking the man out."

"And what could possibly keep me from doing whatever I want to that little pussy?" O'Flaherty asked.

"Only one thing comes to mind. Your bosses."

"My what?"

"Come on, Sean. Don't treat me like a dummy. The big boys, the men of honor. I'm not sure if it's St. Louis or Chicago, but whoever's pulling your strings out here."

"And why the hell would they care what I do to a two-bit punk like Felix?"

It said something about O'Flaherty, though I wasn't sure what, that he didn't even attempt to deny that he was someone's second string.

"Actually," I said, "that's the simplest part to figure. Felix's sob story, falsely accused of murdering his wife's lover, almost fired from the university because of it, has been in the news quite a bit. He's becoming something of a second-string celebrity himself."

O'Flaherty frowned, and some red started creeping around his collar. "All of which means what?"

"All of which means that any extra attention placed on the man, such as if he was gunned down in his home or something like that, would make the news and stoke the story even hotter."

I stopped for a moment and waited for O'Flaherty to object, interrupt, do something. Instead, he merely gave me what I assumed was his steely-eyed glare, calculated to make even a tough guy like me wither away.

Instead, I pushed in even harder. "And so much attention paid to Felix, may eventually lead to you. And I'm guessing the last thing the boys want is for you to be even more public than you are."

He took a deep breath, smoothed the thighs of his pants with his hands, and actually grinned at me.

"Let's say you're right. What's to keep me from biding my time, waiting things out, until the heat dies down. Then doing him in."

"Nothing," I said, "but a lot can happen while you're waiting. I think I've got a better idea."

"Which is?"

I gave him my best shot at the "it's going to be all right" grin. It was an expression I used to use back in the ring, usually right before I sucker punched someone and stomped him into the mat.

"If the good guys can't get to Felix," I said, "and the bad guys, that's you, can't touch him, what say we meet in the middle?"

CHAPTER FORTY-EIGHT

FELIX THAYER LOOKED LIKE A MAN WITHOUT A CARE IN THE WORLD. Stretched out on his dark leather sofa, some sort of soft ambient music playing from his Alexa, and with a nearly-full brandy glass in his hand, he lay with eyes half closed, one hand swaying time to the music. Wearing sharply-pressed khakis and a pink crew neck sweater with his stocking feet up on the other end of the sofa, he presented the perfect picture of a man at ease with his life.

I cleared my throat as loudly as I could, causing him to jerk half upright, brandy swilling out of the glass and onto his sweater. Swiveling his head around, he saw me standing about ten feet behind the couch.

"Quinton!" he barked, voice cracking on the second syllable, "What are you doing here?"

"Seeing how the other half lives," I said.

"How'd you get in?"

"I broke in, through the back door."

Fully upright now, he placed the glass on the coffee table and took a deep breath. "Well, then you can just break right back out. You're not welcome here."

"I wouldn't be so sure about that. Before long, you may be glad that I'm around."

"I doubt that."

Shrugging, I walked over and sat in one of the chairs next to the fireplace. Thayer stood there, looking a little silly and ineffectual. "What are you doing?" he asked after a minute.

"I'm waiting."

"For?"

"You're a smart man, Thayer."

He snorted. "Try brilliant."

"Okay," I conceded, "brilliant. In a short space of time you went from your employment being terminated, not to mention charged with one murder and suspected of another, to coming out of all that smelling like a rose. The cops have nothing to hold against you for either crime, and the last thing they want to do is haul you in again so soon unless they have something rock solid."

"Which obviously they don't. So what?"

"Of course, I'd be willing to bet that the university still wants you gone."

Now we were talking on familiar ground. "Okay, Quinton. I'll play your silly little game. You're right they want me out. But I'd like to see them try now."

"Very true. What would it look like if they axed a man who'd been falsely accused of murder, not to mention just lost his wife in another gruesome murder. They'd look like the most cold-hearted bastards imaginable."

"They would," Thayer said.

"And I'm pretty sure that was a part of your plan from the beginning, along with just proving, at least to yourself, how smart you really are."

"You think I'm going to actually admit to anything?"

"Naw, that's okay. I just want to see how it all plays out. Assuming this was all planned from the beginning, it must have thrown you for a loop when Susan hired me to help you out."

"Why? What the hell would I care about that?"

I was guessing here, and in no way did I expect the man to incriminate himself, but I wanted to throw it out anyway. "Again, just a guess, nothing you have to worry about me being able to prove. But I'm assuming that you had some backstop way of alerting the cops to Abbott. Probably something to do with the two goons that assaulted me in the street."

"You suggesting I hired someone to beat you up?"

"Yeah. Mainly because there's someone else who I first thought had sent them, but I've changed my mind on that. Susan tried to help you without realizing that she was actually screwing up your plan."

He smirked, and I was pretty sure that he'd been dying to gloat to someone, anyone. "If, and let me say again if, you were correct, I'd say the events of the last few days prove your point. I outsmarted you, the cops, even the university brass. So why don't you take your defeat like a man and head on home?"

"You're right," I said, "you've got us all tied up."

Another smirk. Too much more of this and the creep would double over in laughter.

I figured it was time to start lowering the curtain.

"But there's one angle, one group of folks, you overlooked," I said.

"Oh, yeah? What are you going to do? Go to the press with what you know? I'd sue you for everything you have, Quinton. Not that it's that much."

"Not me. When I walk out your door here in a few minutes, my part in all this is over with."

"Then what's your point?"

"You didn't take into account the boys."

"Who?"

I shook my head and leaned forward a bit, placing my arms on my thighs. "Organized crime, Thayer. Genius like you, you didn't factor in the mob."

He frowned, and I could almost see the wheels turning in his head, trying to decipher my meaning. "You're blowing smoke," he said. "What would they want with someone like me?"

"Nothing much," I said, "except that you killed one of their own."

"Huh?"

"You ever heard of a man name of Sean O'Flaherty?" I asked.

"Of course not. Unlike someone such as yourself, I don't hang around with scum and punks."

His words were tough, but the hand that held the brandy glass began shaking a little.

"O'Flaherty's from Chicago," I said. "For the last year or so, he's been the mob's point man here in town."

"Again, so what? You going to make it seem like I took down one of his people in a pathetic attempt to frame me? Really, Quinton, if that's the best you've got—"

"Susan," I said quietly.

"Excuse me?"

"Susan was his cousin."

"I don't—"

"Come on, Thayer. She never talked about her family much, right? Except to say that she was from Illinois? Told you she had a falling out when she was a teenager, am I right? I'm guessing you knew a lot about her first husband, you know, the actual hero. But other than that she probably didn't want to say a lot. Am I right?"

He nodded, his eyes starting to dart around the room.

"And there was the family money she had. Not riches, but enough to live comfortably. I'm guessing you asked more than once about it, but she probably just said something vague and evasive. Maybe even gave you some kind of line like 'what does it matter where it comes from.' Am I right?"

He stayed silent, but his eyes were taking on a sick look.

"The falling out was because most of her family is in organized crime in one way or another. A while back, when the top slot out here opened up, her cousin Sean petitioned to get it. Wanted to be a big fish in a small pond, and keep an eye on his little cousin while he was at it."

"I don't—you can't mean—"

"Cousins, but neither of them have any siblings. 'Cause of that, way I hear it from a reliable source, they're actually about as close as brother and sister. Known each other their whole lives."

"I never—"

"And then you went and got mixed up in all this, and Sean began keeping a close eye, wanting to make sure Susan wouldn't be hurt. He had his boys dogging me every step of the way to see whatever I'd unfold. But after you got scot free out of jail, you went and killed her. How do you think ole' Sean feels about you right about now?"

As he started to get up, I reached into my coat and pulled out my gun.

Thayer froze. "You going to shoot me down, Quinton?"

"Nope. If I wanted to handle you, mister, I could do it with only one hand. The gun's in case anyone else shows up before we finish our talk."

He eased back down onto the couch. "You're making this up?"

"Am I? Her maiden name was Ryan, right? Why don't you spend a little bit of time, if you have it to spend, and do some Googling. You'll see everything I've said is solid."

"What do you mean if I have it to spend?" He was visibly shaking now, so much so that he put down his drink and stared at me with hollow eyes.

"I mean that word on the street is O'Flaherty's coming for you. He and I have actually bumped into each other a couple of times during this thing, so I knew he was involved somehow. I just didn't know how till I did my own Google search. Then I suddenly understood why he was shadowing me the very first day on the case. Why he was looking over my shoulder the whole time. You may be cleared by the cops, at least in terms of what they can prove, and your colleagues may not have much choice but to put up with you a while longer, but O'Flaherty makes his own rules up as he goes along."

"In other words?" the man's voice continued to quaver.

"In other words, you're screwed. You may have a few days before Sean and his boys show up. I'd say it's more like a couple hours. But don't worry. I'll be long gone in a few minutes, then you can handle them on your own."

"You know I can't!" The quaver had turned into an almost screech. "You're talking criminals. Killers."

"What do you think you are? You took out a couple of innocent people on your own. Besides, you're so smart, right? Handling a couple of knuckle-draggers should be no—"

He bolted up now and began heading for the kitchen but made it all of two steps before I clicked back the hammer on my gun. In the silence of the living room, the tiny sound practically boomed, and Thayer pulled himself to a halt.

"What do you want out of me?" he asked with his back to me.

"Personally, Felix, I want nothing from you. I'm practically non-involved in all this. But if I had my preference, I wouldn't like to see O'Flaherty murder anyone, not even a creep like you, so I'll make you a deal."

Thayer's shoulders slumped as he turned back to face me. "What kind of deal? You going to protect me from the Mafia?"

"Of course not. But I will hang around here while you call the cops and turn you over to them. You tell them your story, the real story, and take your chances in the courts."

"That's insane. Why would I do that? All the charges were dropped and I'm free and clear."

At that moment, almost as if planned, came the sound of cars squealing into the driveway and a whole mess of headlights speared into the front windows.

We could hear several car doors opening and closing, and through the draped windows large shadows moved back and forth.

Thayer jumped, his face paling.

"Looks like it wasn't even hours," I said. "My bad. You only had minutes before they came."

A soft but insistent knock sounded at the door.

"What are we going to do?" Thayer whispered

"I'm armed," I said, "and can get you out of here. But only if you go with me to the cops. Other than that, you're on your own."

The professor trembled with indecision.

I stood up. "Okay, then. Handle them yourself."

Before he could answer came another, more insistent knock.

Almost a pounding.

"Get me out of here, Quinton."

"And you'll fess up? To all of it?"

"Yes, God, yes. Just get me out of here."

Holding my weapon in my right hand and grabbing Thayer's elbow in my left, we headed off towards the kitchen area at the back of the house. If we were careful, and lucky, we'd be able to make it through the darkness of the night to my Cherokee, parked down the block and around the corner.

We were and we did.

CHAPTER FORTY-NINE

A COUPLE OF HOURS LATER, I strolled out of the police station and made my way to a small downtown joint that, as I'd told an acquaintance from KC some months back, had the best BBQ in the state. My acquaintance hadn't exactly agreed with me, but she hadn't thrown her food out either.

About half an hour from closing time, the place was almost empty, but the two burly guys hanging around outside, glaring at me as I approached, told me all I needed to know about who was inside.

I glared back at them and walked on in, the after-hours aroma of BBQ cooking all day long darned near overwhelming me.

Sean O'Flaherty sat at a table against the back wall, where he could see anyone who entered, munching on a plate of ribs.

When I walked up, he nodded, gestured towards the empty seat across from him and finished chewing.

"Well?"

"Well, it worked," I said. "Your guys showed up at the house right on time. Thayer's up in the detective bureau now, singing like an opera star."

O'Flaherty nodded and started on the next rib. He didn't offer to share and, with the two bruisers still hanging around outside, I decided not to push it.

"He going to go away?" he asked at one point before digging into a side of macaroni and cheese with bits of bacon sprinkled on top.

"Probably for life. Two murders is nothing to sneeze at. But even if he gets incredibly lucky, he's still looking at between twenty-five and thirty years at the very minimum."

"He know that when he gets out someone'll be waiting for him?"

"I may have neglected to mention that. As it is, he's trembling so much it probably wouldn't have mattered."

"And he doesn't think we can get to him even in prison?" O'Flaherty asked.

I smiled. "Probably hasn't even considered that yet."

"The cops wondering why he's suddenly so cooperative?"

"At the moment, they're not looking a gift horse in the mouth. But if they come around asking later, I'll think of something."

O'Flaherty nodded, wiped his hands with a napkin and pushed his plate to the side. "You done me a favor here, Quinton."

"You got what you wanted, at least partially, and I got what I wanted."

"Don't mean we're buddies or anything."

"No, it doesn't. But I'm guessing I can get up and walk away without the two apes outside taking a swing at me."

O'Flaherty grinned, and for a second there, he looked almost pleasant. "Have a good night, Bomber. See you around."

"God, let's hope not," I said as I got up and headed out.

CHAPTER FIFTY

THE NEXT NIGHT, TALIA SANDERSON AND I got together at Gino's for an early evening pizza, full pitcher of beer and casual conversation. I arrived first and had the beer pitcher on the table and ready, but like a gentleman I'd held off on ordering food until she showed up.

Wasn't easy, but I figured it a small sacrifice to make a good impression. Though it was nothing like the impression the dean made when she opened up the creaky wooden door and walked in.

Against the black and white tiled floor, unvarnished wooden booths and wobbly tables, Dr. Sanderson stood out like a creature from another world.

She'd dressed casual for the occasion, but calling a silk turtleneck sweater, black wool slacks and knee-high leather boots casual was maybe stretching the meaning of the word a bit.

She spotted me right away, no tough feat since Gino's is all of about forty square feet in size and wormed her way into the corner booth I'd chosen.

I poured her a beer.

"You didn't order yet?" she asked.

"Of course not."

She grinned, her teeth showing through. "I wouldn't have minded if you had. Everything they have here is excellent, so you couldn't have gone wrong."

"Come here often?"

Another grin, followed by a light chuckle. "More often than my hips want me to."

In the small amount of time I'd been around her, I hadn't noticed anything wrong with her hips but figured it would be tacky to mention.

We pored over a menu for all of three minutes, and when a young waitress came over to get our order, we went for a large pie, sausage, pepperoni and double mushrooms.

As the girl went off with our order, we engaged in small talk for several minutes before Talia leaned back and gave me a serious look.

"I want to hear all about it," she said.

"About what?"

She shook her head. "Don't play coy with me, Quinton. How does a man with the ego of Felix Thayer, who's practically gotten away with two murders, end up walking into the police station and confessing to both?"

"From what I understand, he didn't walk in. He called the cops and they came to him."

"That's splitting hairs. Far as that goes, from what I get, you were there when the cops picked him up."

"Don't believe everything you hear."

"Uh huh." She paused to take a long sip of her beer, but her eyes never left mine. "You aren't going to tell me a thing, are you?"

"Maybe I can't," I said.

"Don't tell me that, or my curiosity will go through the roof."

I was saved from answering by our food arriving. For a few minutes we chowed down, and I was amazed at how at ease I felt with her. I'm usually a complete barbarian when I eat, especially with my hands, but I worked at being neater than usual.

At least until I noticed she had some sauce dribbled on her chin and didn't seem to mind, at which point I mentally said to hell with it and dug in.

After a period of serious eating where we'd both devoured three slices, we came up for breath.

"I also hear," Talia said, "that he's fired his most recent lawyer and is going court appointed. You know anything about that?"

"No," I said.

"You aren't going to tell me anything, are you?"

I shrugged. "Maybe I'm just keeping kayfabe."

"Say what?"

"Sorry," I said, feeling a bit silly. "It's a term from the wrestling business. From way back, even before I got started. It means that you do your best to make sure the crowd believes all the fake stuff going on in the ring. Keeping kayfabe means that you carry on afterwards just the same."

"I don't follow."

"It's like this. Let's say that your opponent you're facing tonight, who works for the same company you do, is one of your best friends."

"Okay."

"But to get the crowd jazzed up, you act like he's your worst enemy. You want to rip his head off because he stole your girl, or something like that. Make sense so far?"

"As much as it possibly can."

I grimaced at her commentary. "To make it really realistic, after you've bloodied each other up but good in the ring, you can't go out to a bar after and have a drink together, because what if some fans saw the two of you having a grand old time. The illusion from the ring would have been broken."

"Even though everyone knows that stuff's a put on."

"Well, sure. Nowadays. But back in the old days, I mean really far back, probably half of the fans if not more believed it was all true."

"So you did your best to—how did you say it—keep kayfabe?"

"That's about it."

She looked about to ask me a follow up, then reversed course. "Tell you what," she said. "How about I stop trying to talk shop with you and we both just enjoy the hell out of this meal."

I grinned. "Sounds like a plan."

"At least the first step of one."

"Huh?"

"Well, hell Quinton. At the rate we're going, the two of us will have this table cleared in another fifteen minutes or so."

"Yeah?"

"That's going to leave a whole lot of the night before us. I sure hope you have more than one step in your plan."

"Give me a minute," I said, "while I work something out."

"Don't strain yourself. If you don't have any ideas, I've got one or two of my own."

Yep, I thought, enough of the stop talk.

I couldn't wait to see what kind of steps she had in mind.

A HIGH-SCHOOL TEACHER, FORMER COLLEGE INSTRUCTOR AND fiction writer, Kevin R. Doyle is the author of numerous short stories, mainly in the horror field. He's also written three crime thrillers, *The Group, When You Have to Go There,* and *And the Devil Walks Away* and one horror novel, *The Litter*. Recently, he's begun working on the Sam Quinton private eye series. The first Quinton book, *Squatter's Rights*, was nominated for the 2021 Shamus award as Best First PI Novel. The second book, *Heel Turn*, was released in March of 2021. More information can be found at kevindoylefiction.com.

www.ingramcontent.com/pod-product-compliance
Lightning Source LLC
Chambersburg PA
CBHW011516100726
47899CB00010BD/3396

* 9 7 8 1 6 8 4 9 2 0 1 2 9 *